# The Day Nobody Died

an Arcadia Vyne Mystery

by

## Ira Amos

# James Kay Publishing

## Tulsa, Oklahoma

The Day Nobody Died

ISBN 978-1-943245-73-4

*In Memory of*
*Arcadia Vyne's First Fan*
*Becky Bozich*


*Special Thanks*
*to Carolyn*

*Beloved, do not avenge yourselves, but rather give place to wrath; for it is written,*
*"Vengeance is Mine, I will repay," says the Lord.*

Romans 12:19 (NKJV)

# The Players
in alphabetical order

Sergeant Griz Asher

Mr. Holbrook Thompson Bahr

Miss Janet Bahr

Baylee
(the chauffeur)

Mr. Jonas Cooper

Miss Ava Erdody

Mr. Elias Erdody

Gus
(a thug)

Ma
(Tommy Ray & Billy's mother)

"Hubby" Mundene

Millicent B. Mundene

Mr. Gerald Myton

Mr. Arthur Myton

Mr. & Mrs. Thorndike Neufeld

Mr. & Mrs. Cuthbert Preston III

Miss Rowena Preston

Detective Burgess Raft

Tommy Ray & Bobby
(the cowboys)

Mr. Rodrick
(the secretary)

Brock "Sandman" Sanderson

Miss Mary Smith
(the librarian)

Stewart
(the valet)

Mr. Arcadia Vyne

Deputy Beuford Warner

Willoughby
(a ticket agent)

# Denver, Colorado
## Elev. 5280

# ONE

Here's a tip when you're trying to pick a guy's mug out in a police lineup. Forget about the loud ugly tie he's wearin' and concentrate on some tell or feature which makes him stand out from the others. A scar. A twitchy lip. Cauliflower ear. Hawk nose. Chipped tooth. Wart. Mole. Tic. Droopy eye. Gimpy leg. Missing arm. You get the picture.

This lineup offered none of the above, but one little indiscriminate giveaway was all I needed to peg this guy as the one who planted his fist in the middle of Mary Smith's pretty little nose.

And yes *that is* her name.

The cute librarian I sometimes go Dutch with at Pug's when we're both in the mood for some of his diner-style strawberry rhubarb pie. Mary won't be having any strawberries or rhubarbs for a while unless the hospital serves them to her through a straw. Hard to eat pie with your jaw wired shut.

Now, you can understand why it was so important for me to put the touch on the right guy in this pick of the crop from Denver's gray bar inn for ne'er-do-wells, rogues, mischievants, vagrants, and vagabonds.

No doubt Detective Burgess Raft had a couple of his cops infiltrate the line. At least two of the five were having trouble mimicking the mannerisms of their daily foes.

To do it right, Raft shouldn't even have been in the room. He should have set this up as a 'double blind' so as to not unintentionally influence my selection. He should have informed me of how the real perpetrator might or might not be present and that he does not know which person is the suspect. At two o'clock in the morning he should have been home asleep.

Of course, I knew the detective could care less if he unintentionally influenced my selection about as much as he cared if I had my corned beef on rye or pumpernickel or with a side of cabbage.

As to the perpetrator being present....

The cement below the five pairs of footwear exposed a smooth and shiny path made from all of the previous boots and shoes of all the previous lineups and showups from who knows how far back in the jail's history. The new jail wouldn't be ready for guests until sometime in '39. Some of these rogues probably had their reservations set for the grand opening.

But not contestants Two and Three in this beauty competition. They had black service leather shoes which were just as shiny as where they stood. Too shiny for this row. I expect all but one could even afford $1.49 for a pair if they weren't part of the uniform. Hence Mug One and Mug Four in their Salvation Army footwear moved to the head of the class as most likely to pound their grandmother into unconsciousness for a sawbuck. Mug Five had on two-toned Oxfords and would do it for a five spot. But that didn't count as a tell.

"Okay, Cooper. You see the guy?" Raft turned up the collar of his overcoat. Despite this being June, the half dark room felt a bit chilly, and I don't mean in a twilight sort of way, but in a way where our end of the cave hid in the dark and the opposite

end of the cave, with the faded lines of height mark-
ings on the wall, lit up like a used car lot. It also
smelled damp like a wet dog after a swim in the
pond.

"I'm lookin'."

"Any of these jamokes put your girlfriend in
traction?"

"She ain't my girlfriend."

"Girlfriend or not, any genius who'd do what he
did to her has gotta be dumber than a cup of coffee.
How'd he get past you?"

I tipped my hat forward and reached to test the
knot on the back of my skull. "He clocked me from
behind with what I can only describe as a fire hy-
drant."

"Then he beat her up?" Raft pulled his tobacco
pouch and Chesterfield pipe from an inner pocket.
"Sending you a message?"

"If he did, I didn't understand —"

The second guy in line scuffed the heel of his
shoe on the floor and grunted.

Mug One yelled, "When we gonna get some
chow?"

"Shut up, you clowns! Breakfast ain't scrambled
'til six." The stunted Detective Raft turned to his
bear of a right-hand man. "Griz, next one of them

peeps, you clamp a fist around his throat so tight he'll need an eyedropper to eat gravy."

Sergeant Griz Asher snickered. "With pleasure!" He said it loud enough for all in the room to hear for at least four echoes. "Back up, number one. Everybody turn! To the right, crumb! Show me those profiles real easy like and they better not be smilin' or I'll wipe 'em off your faces with my fist."

"How about it, Cooper?" Raft whispered as if to protect my identity.

Then I spotted it. The slightest twitch of the cheek as Mug Five dared Sergeant Asher to classify his smirk as a grin. In the not too distant past this greaseball had knelt down to stare at me on the ground. Showed me his bloody fist with strands of Mary's hair between the knobby fingers. The smirk. I had him dead to rights. Maybe I did see those two-tones from the worm's eye view. But the smirk was the tell.

"Well?"

"Fella who attacked us.... Not in this bunch."

"What!" Detective Raft's incredulity made him drop the match he'd just lit. It sputtered and extinguished itself on the damp floor. "Look again!"

"Face forward, you lot! Now, your left. Okay, you comedian, your other left!" Asher covered the

ten steps to the lighted end of the room and man-
handled each one around in turn. All the men's
heads stood just below the faded five-foot-eight line
on the wall. All the men had the same build. All the
men wore loud ugly ties.

Mug Five had just the right smirk to qualify as
my new best enemy.

"Like I said, he ain't in this lot, Detective. You
can send 'em all back to the tank. Except for the
two cops."

Raft nodded. "Forgot you're a former badge.
You've done this before from where I'm standing,
haven't you?"

"And from where they're standing too. Funny
how many crooks I resembled back in the day."

"I'll remember that next time it rains." The stem
of his pipe pointed at the lineup. "He's there, Jonas.
Tag him and let's go home."

Now, it was getting personal, what with Raft
calling me by my given name and all. They'd let
Mug Five wash the blood off his fists and both the
detective and the sergeant knew who was who.

Everybody in the room knew who was who.

I certainly knew who was who.

"Don't be makin' this a trip for biscuits." Griz
Asher tilted his head to the side until neck bones

cracked. "Point him out, Cooper. Me and the boys will handle the rest."

"I tell you the fella who spoiled Mary's evening is not in this dance."

Raft peered up at me through his black rimmed-glasses, took hold of my arm, and stepped me further back in the room. "Let's go over this again, Cooper."

"Look, I know the routine. I've made my statement. I've told my story to your bear, Asher. I've told my story to you."

"Tell it again. Chapter and verse."

"We were standing on the southwest corner of 5th Avenue and Lincoln."

"What were you doing there?"

"Look—"

"Tell it again."

"Detective—"

"Again, Cooper!"

Someone in the lineup guffawed.

The sound of Griz Asher's backhand interrupted the joviality and echoed between the walls.

I took a deep breath. "Okay, from the start. I met Mary at the Diamond Ballroom after her shift at the library. She came straight over. I'd been at Pug's putting away some of his coffee."

"You currently on a case?"

"No."

"Anything recent?"

"Couple of things."

"Such as?"

"Vyne has me working on some stuff."

Raft sighed. "Arcadia Vyne. I'd hoped you shake loose from that eccentric beanpole."

"He keeps me on retainer. I'm living in an apartment over his carriage house at the moment." I didn't have the heart to tell Raft that Vyne considered him eccentric as well.

"This stuff you're working on? What?" A match snicked off Raft's thumbnail in the dim light and the flame hovered near the bowl of his Chesterfield pipe like a little shimmering ghost. "Meddle in anything rough lately?"

"Far from it. Neighbor's missing dog. Someone stole three hubcaps off the bank president's car."

The loud belly laugh which emitted from the detective startled everyone in the room.

"It's not funny, Raft." I meant it.

"Dogs and hubcaps?" He shook his head from side to side "Dogs and hubcaps. Really, Cooper if you don't see the humor. Have you stooped so low?" He swept the room with a wave of his hand. "We may all be good cops and are doing our job well, but surely you can find some crime out there more befitting your station in life."

"I've been in a bit of slump."

"I'll say."

"Do you want me to go on or not — "

"Hey, when do we get some chow?"

"Don't get your gauges up!" yelled Sergeant Asher.

"But — "

"Shut up!"

Raft took a step toward the lineup. "Our men can stand down, Sergeant. Cooper made them the minute he walked in here."

The two contestants lowered their heads as if ashamed of their failure to look more criminal.

"The other three clowns can sit in the corner while we sort this out over here."

"Yes, sir." Asher pointed at the floor. "Sit!"

"How 'bout some chow, man? We're starvin'." The first in line rubbed his belly. "I tell you we're starvin'."

Raft turned his attention back to me and puffed his pipe. "Diamond Ballroom. You met Mary. What next?"

"Mary had mentioned she wanted to hear

Sammy Kaye's Orchestra play *Rosalie*. I wanted to go to the show and see *The Adventures of Robin Hood* at the Fox Mayan. Turns out she's no fan of Errol Flynn. She's cute and she wins the coin toss. I know a guy who knows a guy at the Diamond who fixed me up with a table close to the brass. Mary likes to dance. I'm not so hot at it but figured why not."

"You step on anyone's toes?"

"Just Mary's."

"Go on."

"We sat out *Carolina Moon*, and then I made like a cement mixer to *Hurry Home*. Got a cramp in my foot and we decided to leave. She was hungry, and a friend had told her the Pioneer Room at the Cosmopolitan Hotel served up a tasty Waldorf salad."

"You were going to spring forty cents on a salad for someone who is *not* your girlfriend? Vyne must be paying you pretty good to hunt down missing dogs and hubcaps."

"Yesterday was her birthday."

Raft took a breath. "Sorry. You failed to mention that before. Rotten thing to end up in the hospital on your birthday. Anything else you failed to mention when you conveyed this yarn the first time?"

"I don't think so."

"Okay, go on."

"After I stood around awhile and worked the cramp out of my foot, we made for the door. Mary went to powder her nose and after that we sauntered out onto the sidewalk."

"Would you know if she mentioned anything worth mentioning while out of your sight? Maybe she gave one of these losers the cold shoulder?" He pointed to the trio of rats on the floor. "Insult one of their wives?"

"No, she seemed just fine. No different than when she went in. Besides what woman would let any of those comedians put a ring on their finger?"

"You think she was the target? Or, was it random? After you? Sending a message to Vyne?"

"I don't know. He didn't take her purse."

"Now, there is something helpful."

"I suppose."

"Your wallet?" He waved off the thought when I produced it from my inner coat pocket. "Fireplugs aside, what do you think he clubbed you with?"

"Not a lead pipe. Board?" I reached to the knot on my head again and winced. "Something with a smaller striking surface. Glanced off. Hammer maybe."

"We found a claw hammer nearby."

"You failed to mention *that* before."

"You didn't ask. Makes us even. Besides, no usable fingerprints. Remember anything before you got glanced? See anyone homing in on you? Hear anything?"

"Mary screamed."

"Well, seeing someone come at a guy, who's taking her to buy a salad, with a hammer will cause a woman to do that."

"Probably means she didn't recognize him."

"You sure it wasn't a dame who clocked you?"

"No dame put Mary in a hospital bed."

"Good point." Raft puffed his pipe some more, then walked over to his sergeant. "Line these three clowns up again."

The jailbirds took their place and Raft motioned me to the edge of the light.

"He's not here." Mug Three, formerly Mug Five, smirked again. I memorized his face.

Raft sighed. "One and Two go back to their cells, Griz. Make sure they don't keep the ties. Send the ugly clown back to his circus."

Asher protested. "They're all ugly as the day is long."

When the troupe cleared the door, I stepped into the bright light. "I'm sorry, Raft, I—"

"Look, Cooper. We had a doorman at the

Diamond see the whole thing. Built like a tank."

"I remember him. Couldn't button his coat."

"That's the one. He even tried to pull the guy off Mary Smith. Got the hammer in the throat for his troubles. That made him real mad. When he could breathe again, he gave chase for two full blocks. Right into a patrolman's fender. Took both my man and the tank to get the joker to the ground. His fists were covered in blood." A curl of smoke circled the detective's head like an ethereal shark.

Ever since I started going out with a librarian, I'd taken to reading the dictionary.

"You just let him walk out of here. What gives?"

"He wasn't the guy."

Raft waved me off. "Hogwash. You weren't seeing straight."

"If your two-ton track star had the guy, why not have said track star spot him in the lineup?"

"When the doorman got a really good look, he turned from Jesse Owens into Harpo Marx. Seems the sight of an ugly clown put the fear in him so bad his lips sewed shut. Now, it looks like the same ugly clown has put the fear in you..."

To say that hurt my feelings is an understatement.

"...and I find that very disappointing." Raft

picked up a file folder from the desk by the door and stuck it under my nose. "Prints say his name is Sanderson. Brock 'Sandman' Sanderson, aka Sandy Sanderson, aka Brock Sanders. Muscle from east of the big river. Nothing outstanding. Therefore, I can't hold him. We get a sheet on 'em when they move around a lot, so we already had a running start on making an ID. First we've seen of him here in Denver and I'd like to get his sideshow off the street. The street you just put him back on."

I shrugged. "What can I say?"

That was a mistake.

Raft came unglued and slapped the folder on the desk. Then he pointed his pipe at the clock over the door. "You see what time it is? Two-twenty. In the morning, Cooper. You have wasted half my night. Half my night. And for what? A smug little shrug."

I shrugged again. Couldn't help it.

The detective leaned back and pointed a finger up into my chest. "Get out of my station, Cooper! If I hear of you so much as parking too far from the curb, I'll have you buried down in the tombs with the bad tie gang."

"I don't drive."

This caused the sheaf of papers to fly out of the folder as Raft flung his arms about. "For Pete's sake, somebody get this bum out of my station before I get *myself* arrested!"

This seemed to be where the line could be crossed no further. I tipped my hat and made for the door. "*Adieu*, Detective Raft. Tell Sargent Asher to drop dead and I'll tell the Professor you want to be invited over to his *casa* for tea."

"I don't like tea and I don't like Arcadia Vyne more than I don't like tea!"

I felt the folder hit me in the back but thought better of pursuing the banter any further this dreary morning. It was early. I was tired. I hadn't had any coffee in a while. I figured Sergeant Asher had stuffed my raincoat in a wastebasket and I had a man to find.

# Two

My nose for rain proved true to form. If you called the drizzly mess, falling out of the sky through the yellowish light coming from the windows of the Denver Police Department this morning, rain. Some people probably did. So, keeping to the shadows at the top of the steps, I did too.

In addition to finding my raincoat, the scavenger hunt delayed me a bit as I had to reclaim my .32 revolver they'd taken off me when I'd been wobblin' around tryin' to get away from the knot on the back of my head. It was now tucked in my shoulder holster where it belonged.

Larimer St., with its number 64 track lines, looked to be deserted except to the north. About a block up between 15th and 16th a body leaned against a lamppost on the opposite side of the street, across from the Manufacture's Building, and lit a cigarette.

I couldn't be so lucky.

But when Brock Sanderson, aka Mug Three, formerly Mug Five, shifted his weight my way and arched his back to exhale a mouthful of smoke up into the light.... It was that ugly tie. Even from a block away, through the drizzle, under a weak lamp, I could identify that nasty flap of bedsheet like I could see the sun on a cloudless day.

Things were looking up. I'd originally planned to pack ice on the back of my noggin and crawl under the warm covers up in the carriage house apartment. In the morning, after a couple of coffees, and, yes, even though Arcadia Vyne is the heir to a tea empire, he does allow his personal valet, Stewart, a bit of leeway in brewing me something you can't read a newspaper through. Silent Stewart did everything for Vyne, from maintaining his clothes, to running his bath, to shaving his chin. He did none of the above for me, except said coffee brewing, but I didn't sign his paycheck, did I?

Anyway, after a couple of cups of Stewart's bean juice, I'd make some calls and find out what scummy rock Sanderson the Sandworm hid himself under. Then I'd go see him and explain with my dukes how much Mary didn't like being in the hospital. How much she didn't like having her jaw wired shut. How much she didn't like his really ugly tie.

But this bit of fortune chucked that plan into the can.

Waiting to see which way Sanderson would go, I stayed at the top of the steps until he buttoned his coat and pulled his hat over his brow. Doing the same and being sure he had started walking away from me and down the opposite of Larimer, I descended the steps and soon loitered in front of Fire Station #6.

The dampness seemed to draw out the stable smell from the bricks as in earlier years the first floor housed not only the fire wagons, but stalls of horses. The fire boys lived up on the second floor in what had probably been a hay loft and tack room. Now, instead of the whinny of horses came the snores of tired men through the open awning windows above.

Hopefully my luck would hold, and the alarm

would not sound, and the tired men would not evacuate their beds for a ride down the brass poll. They wouldn't be putting harnesses on anything or revving up those big gas engines.

I didn't need the limelight to come down on me. Not while I had Sanderson in my sights.

He crossed back to my side, and I noticed a slight limp in his gait. In hindsight I did remember him ever so slightly favoring one leg over the other in the lineup. He stopped in front of the Manhattan Restaurant to read their menu posted by the door. After a moment, he ran his fingers along the edge of the frame and tilted it up just enough to get a hand behind it. What he retrieved remained a mystery as it disappeared under the lapel of his coat.

Had Sanderson stashed it there earlier, or did someone leave it as a drop?

With a pat on said lapel, as if satisfied with his find, he walked to the corner of 17th at the Continental Building.

If he continued north, I didn't know where he was going. If he turned left, I had a pretty good idea he'd be heading for Union Station. I crossed 15th unable to avoid ankle deep puddles and hesitated in front of the Fred Davis Furniture Company.

Now, my socks felt like sponges in my shoes. I really don't like wet socks.

Left won the dark morning as he headed toward the sound of freight trains. His pace quickened by a half step.

I kept to the shadows and passed the old Service Men's Dormitory, then John H. Dyson, Desher Cigars, and Jason Williams shoes.

When I made 17th I saw Sanderson had crossed to the far side of the street again. He was midway between the Alamo and St. Elmo Hotels and continued walking at a jaunt like he hadn't a care in his big bad world.

Wet socks kept me from such jaunty footwork.

There still wasn't anyone else on the streets, not even a moving car or truck, although I could hear the occasional blast of a horn echo between the buildings. There were plenty of parked vehicles, and they made good cover, but you could get yourself in a trouble if someone up for a glass of water took a gander out of one of those hotel windows and decided you were committing a crime on one of those said vehicles. Especially if it belonged to them. I've heard it's the nosey ones who can't mind their own business who most often put the foul-up on a tail.

I really didn't have a lot of experience in shadowing someone. T-town just never presented a case where I had the reason to do so. Downtown Denver covered a lot more real estate, both in width, depth, and height.

The trick seemed to be to decide if I needed to stay on a loose tail or tighten it up. If Sanderson kept his beeline to Union I didn't need to get silly about it. If he ducked into the lobby of one of the hotels, I'd have to hop to it.

As I finished crossing Market St. and stepped under the awning of the Mine & Smelter Supply Co.'s main entrance, where it smelled like grease and old rags, it dawned on me that this might not be a cold tail.

Sanderson could in fact be a warm subject if he suspected I was following him. Or, he might have already burned me and knew for sure. He had just a bit too much of a casual air about him as he crossed Blake St., then Wazee, past the Hendrie & Botlhoff Mining Machinery Company, and finally Wynkoop St. to enter the station.

I thought back to the streetlamp. This jellybean should have been long gone. Had he waited on me? Wanted me to follow him? The back of my head throbbed as I considered what he was up to.

Then, I considered what he hadn't done in the proceeding blocks.

He hadn't stopped to tie his shoe.

Picked up a gum wrapper.

Stared into a store window.

Ducked into an alley.

Nonchalantly looked back.

Shouted, "Hey, I see you!"

Threw lead at me.

No. He had stopped to read that menu.

Checked out a clock over a jeweler's shop.

Compared it to his watch.

Tossed his cigarette in the flowing gutter.

He had not lit another one.

Instead, he made it straight for the train station.

Either he didn't know I was behind him.

Or, he did.

A fifty-fifty chance stood in the rain between me and Union Station.

# THREE

Tailing a guy who is about to get on a train can be awkward. But by now I'd decided he knew I was behind him or he intentionally wanted me to be behind him. Either way, it looked as if we were about to leave the Mile High city by rail.

I'd had a similar experience back on the force when they sent me to the Big Easy to extradite a gorilla of a fella back to Tulsa who'd made a withdrawal with a .38 and deposited some lead into a teller. This fella proceeded to head south to drink up some of his loot on Bourbon Street and ended it by beaning a cop with a bottle. This earned him a stay at the expense of the New Orleans' taxpayers and they wanted no more of him when his wanted poster crossed the desk of Captain Mason Guillory. As the parish police pulled off the crumb's bracelets to exchange them for mine, the chucklehead decided to compound his troubles and slugged his way out the front door. Didn't help that the streets of the French Quarter were packed with looky-loos. We managed to chase him onto a Canal streetcar where he held the driver hostage for about three blocks until the car lurched on the tracks and the idiot fell out the open door. Luckily, he managed to break his fall in two places with his arm.

Best thing about that trip - the gumbo and the grits.

You order either gumbo or grits in Denver and they look at you like your ear fell off.

This guy this morning on his way to the agent's counter, Sanderson, had migrated from back east and I'd bet my old harmonica against your new one that the guy didn't like gumbo either. He pocked his ticket and headed for the brightly lit platform. Made him easy to see as everything else to the north, south, and west painted a midnight black, save for a few streetlights.

My stomach reminded me of a missed meal.

Thoughts of gumbo and grits have a tendency to do that. It didn't help that a sign in the shape of a fish advertised: Mountain Trout Every Day in the Dining Car.

At the counter I, most likely the second customer at this hour, asked the baby-faced kid with a mustache older than his peach fuzz, "Where's the last ticket heading?"

"I really don't think that is any of your business," came the reply from under the hairy brush.

"Give me a twin to the same place." I pushed a Walking Liberty half dollar forward under the bars but kept my finger on the old girl's face. "Same place as that guy and I won't look while this falls in your pocket."

The young agent licked his bottom lip. "Laramie."

"We get there before daylight?"

He glanced up at a board and then pulled a pocket watch to consult and compare. "Yes, sir."

I liked the politeness and lifted my finger from the coin. "How many cars?"

"This one's a long haul, usually seven passenger, baggage, sleeper, dining car, plus the freight. Never know how many they tack on. It'll be about half full of folks. Most of 'em heading on up to Jackson Hole.

Some from the big rodeo down in Colorado Springs."

That suited me just fine.

The mustached agent licked the lower lip again and raised his neck as if his gaze might see into my pocket. He looked like a brat anticipating a candy. "Anything else I can help you with, sir?"

"Dining car going to be open? I got a hankerin' for trout."

"No," he glanced at the clock. "It'll be closed for the night."

"Figures."

"Anything else?"

"A ticket."

"Oh, yeah. Two dollars."

"I edged a five spot his way."

He produced said ticket, three silver simoleons in change, and I tipped my hat.

If Sanderson chose a car toward the front of the train, I'd wait and pick one a few back. If the middle, then the same plan. If the back, I'd have no other choice than to sit ahead of him. Either way, every bit of the train went in the same direction and made the same stops. Besides, if he'd been wise to me all along, it didn't really matter.

Of course, I could just jump him here on the

platform. There were a couple of four-wheeled baggage carts and some crates for cover. At least I'd be in Raft's jurisdiction and the old so-and-so might cut me some slack for making a mess of someone he didn't want in his town. On the other hand, something about the wide-open spaces of Wyoming where the wild west still meant something appealed to me. Normally I'm a pretty docile fellow. Rather settle things with brains than brawn. But the continued throbbing of the knot on my noggin and the thought of Mary Smith's pretty face being not so pretty at the moment fueled a rage down in my gut that nothing less than bloody knuckles would satisfy. Mine, not his.

Three more sleepy travelers appeared and parked their luggage near the tracks.

A light to the south grew larger and larger until it led its diesel engine past the platform and presented a selection of cars. The conductor opened the door to the first Pullman as the train glided to an abrupt halt. This threw my plan to the wind as no other conductor with no other door did the same. With just five passengers including Sanderson and myself, the choice of boarding narrowed to just the one car.

At this point I considered simply sitting next to

the guy and glaring at him all the way to Laramie, but he paid me no mind and never looked back as he assured the conductor he traveled without luggage before limping down the aisle, thumping his hands on the backs of the opposing seats on his way to the next car. Needless to say, those sleeping in those seats protested each and every thump. Sanderson wanted all the passengers, including me, to know he was on board, and he controlled the time and the place.

Circumstances settled for the moment, I slid into a deep cushioned reclining seat facing the rear of the luxurious car and tried my best for the next hour not to fall asleep to the clickity-clack of the wheels below.

Heading up the Denver Pacific line, we stopped briefly at Greeley but no passengers disembarked. Across the state line, at Cheyenne, several people got off and I opened my window so I could see the platform better. Sanderson didn't join them. Soon we were switched to tracks heading west and were on our way again.

Finally, the train pulled into the Laramie Depot and this time I stepped onto the platform before anyone else and made my way to a trio of pine trees to the south. Sanderson got off last after a couple of cowboy-looking types and made his way to the north end of the platform and around the corner of the red brick depot.

I assumed the two young men were cowboys because they carried saddles.

Darkness still held the night, and I made my way around the south end. A sedan's engine coughed to life, its headlights suddenly illuminating the back of the depot, and Sanderson wasted no time crawling into the passenger seat.

Sometimes not driving a car can be a hindrance, but it didn't matter at the moment, for there wasn't another car anywhere I could drive if I wanted to. Which I didn't.

Then a pickup, which looked like it might have been the very first off Henry Ford's assembly line, chugged up and the two cowboy types tossed their trail worn saddles in the bed.

I whistled and got their attention. "Hey, you boys want to earn some coin for your pocket?"

"Some what?" The taller of the two spit tobacco juice on the rear wheel. "Who are you?"

"I got a silver dollar for all three of you if you'll follow the sedan that just left and let me ride along in the truck's bed."

The shorter of the two rubbed his hands on his

jeans. "Why, shore, mister. We'll take your money. Hop in."

"Hey!" yelled an aged female voice from the cab. "What are you boys doin' back there?"

"Don't worry 'bout it, Ma. We got a passenger."

"A passenger?" The driver's side door opened, and a dingy cab light illuminated a head of stringy gray hair.

"Don't get out, Ma. He's in a hurry," the short one said. "You want us ta catch it?"

I shook my head. "Just follow."

"We can do that." He motioned to the taller one. "Hop back here with this fella, Tommy Ray."

I pulled my hat down tight and we hopped.

"See this dude don't fall out." He made his way to the driver's door. "Scoot over, Ma! I'm drivin'."

"How was yall's trip, boy? What's that feller doin' hitchin' a ride in the middle of the night?"

"Fine, Ma. Ain't none of our business, Ma. Jus' a bit of a side trip." He reached a hand out the window and slapped the door. "Hang on back there, you two."

With that, the sound of gears grinding brought a protest from the matriarch of the pair. "I thought I told you to get the clutch fixed, boy!"

We traveled about ten yards in second gear

when the pickup lurched to a stop. "Hey, mister," came a voice from the driver's side. "Ma says since you're payin' you're riden' up front with us."

"That's okay. I'm fine back here." I'd latched onto a rusty wheel hub which had probably been tossed into the bed during the Calvin Coolidge administration. "Can you still see his taillights?"

"Suit yourself." The truck lurched into gear again. "Looks like he's headin' out toward the Station," came a yell over the engine.

I tapped Tommy Ray on the shoulder. "What's 'the Station'?"

"Used to be a prison. Now the university uses it to do livestock and crop research."

The night breeze shifted and the unmistakable waft of all things cattle brought back memories of hanging around the stockyards in my youth.

In the little moonlight available, the outline of the old prison looked foreboding. A place where rough men were given an even rougher place to pay their debt to society. Dark rock walls. Heavy timbered doors. Barn odors carried along thoughts of distress and desperation and mingled in the night air as they mixed with the dirty debris of the desert. Heavy with the burden, the breeze picked up into a light wind.

The car containing Sanderson slowed and turned into a service road a dozen yards or so beyond the old prison. Headlights faded out and the vehicle proceeded by apparent familiarity of the road under its tires.

The pickup stopped and I tapped on the dirty cracked back glass of the cab. "Kill your engine and lights."

Without complaint, all went silent and dark.

Out here from the city, I could see a lot of stars.

Cicadas chirped, but not enough to keep me from hearing the sedan rev its motor a few times before dying just beyond eyesight and around the corner of the large main structure.

I pulled myself over the side of the pickup's dented bed and the dirt road under my shoes sent a shock of numbness through my knees and into my spine. Steadying myself, I moved to the open passenger's side window and got my first look at the matriarch of the cowboy twins. Even in shadow, the weathered Wyoming wrinkles lay in furrows of testimony to the rodeo life she'd lived.

"What now, mister?" She pushed a dip of snuff into her lower lip. "This ain't no place you want to be tonight."

"Agreed." I looked past the hood of the truck.

"One of those in that car put a fist in a friend's face and this is as good a place as any to deal some justice. She might not agree, but —"

"She?"

"She. And a librarian no less."

Ma spit out the window and just missed my shoe. "Why, those good for nothin'.... Bobby, you go with this fella and take your shotgun."

Bobby appeared all too eager to do as told. He quickly had the weapon out of the window rack and fished down in the fold of the seat for what I assumed might be the shells.

"No." I held up a palm. "This is my fight. Don't want anyone else to get hurt." The thought of getting hurt myself didn't hold much appeal. The older I get, the more I value my teeth.

"Suit yourself." Ma seemed relieved the honor of her son had been put on the line but wouldn't be tested. "Want we should stay? When you're finished we can give you a ride back to wait for the next train."

"You three live anywhere close?"

"Base of the Snowies." Bobby pointed west with the shotgun. "Thirty-five miles or so."

"Fair enough." I motioned them on. "Be daylight soon. I'll walk back."

"Suit yourself," Ma repeated. "Bobby, nudge this ol' thing in neutral and roll down the way. At least those yonder might think this fellers got somebody out here backin' him up."

"But, Ma." Bobby re-racked his weapon. "We can't just go off an —"

"Hush, boy! This fella knows what he's doin'."

"You think so?" I asked.

She let another spit fly. "I got a sense about you, mister. You take up for your lady friend."

I fished the silver dollars from my pocket and handed them to Bobby.

He handed one to Tommy Ray, one to his sweet mother, and put the third between his teeth to test its authenticy.

Ma winked. "Kick 'em an extra time for me."

Sounded good as I watched them head for the Snowies.

Ten minutes later I had made my way to an exterior wall of the biggest building. It appeared to be constructed of some type of light gray sandstone set in a random pattern. At least it appeared gray as it reflected the meager moonlight. Everything below waist level looked more deteriorated than the counterpart wall reaching to a couple of stories above. The corner of the building sported larger reddish-brown finished masonry blocks, and this is from where I peered through some cattle pens to a secondary building.

The sedan sat in front of a set of double barn doors and light flooded from the windows of the structure. Two voices carried above the snorting of sleeping livestock, but not loud enough to discern words.

I worked my way to below one of the windows. The breeze had lessened again but kicked up enough to carry a paper of some sort from the open door to against my thigh.

My fingers grabbed it, and the feel felt familiar. Tilting the paper to the yellowish light I read:

BULLETIN NO. 227                    JUNE 1938

UNIVERSITY OF WYOMING
## AGRICULTURAL
## EXPERIMENT STATION
SUGAR BEET TOPS, COTTONSEED
CAKE, AND MONO-CALCIUM
PHOSPHATE IN RATIONS
FOR STEERS

Not everyone's idea of bedtime reading to be sure. To top it off, the University of Wyoming must have a huge printing budget as this paper stock didn't seem to be your run of the mill County Agent handout.

What it normally held in print; I couldn't put my finger on. *Something important, but what?*

As if on cue to answer my conundrum, a loud clackety machine went to work.

I'd heard it before.

Printing press.

What did Sanderson need with bulletins exalting the merits of 'Rations for Steers'?

Maybe they were bootlegging cattle feed. This, I had to see.

# Four

The night breeze picked up a bit and tumble-weeds tumbled up against my leg in the dark. Big ones. Small ones. The first one unnerved me a bit as I thought it might have teeth. Sharp teeth backed up with glowing eyes and a set of claws. I half expected it to howl in a sort of telegraph way to call all the other yipping four legged nocturnals to join it for a meal.

Between the distant lyrical high-pitched barks carried on the breeze, the chirping cicadas, and the snoring cattle, the darkness played a symphony highlighted by a passing crackle and wispy swoosh of said tumbling tumbleweeds.

Interrupted intermittently when the two goons inside the building set their printing press in motion.

When they did so, I removed my hat and chanced raising up to look through the dingy window, knowing their attention would be on the machine.

Sanderson did a lot of watching. The other guy, who wore a leather apron, did a lot of moving back and forth.

Whatever they were duplicating in there, they were duplicating a lot of it.

Every now and then the machine stopped, and the operator did some fiddling with it. Sanderson inspected the paper product closely under a hanging bulb. Apparently satisfied they were nearing perfection, he removed a brown envelope, which I surmised he must have retrieved from behind the framed menu at the Manhattan, from his inside coat pocket and extracted a document of some type. I wondered if it might be printed on the same kind of paper going through the press. Grabbing a magnifying glass from a shelf, he selected a random sheet of their freshly printed creation, placed them side-by-side on a table, and moved the glass back and forth between them.

When Sanderson finally looked up at the press operator, his big grin confirmed things were a go. "Looks like you've got the ink mix figured out."

The printer operator nodded and wiped his hands on a rag. "That last calibration did the trick."

With them focused on their efforts and me focused on them, I failed to hear or see the third goon who focused on me. My first indication was his big meaty fingers coming around my throat from behind. My second was as he lifted me about six inches off the ground. My third was when he used my forehead to tap on the window.

"Hey boss!" The big thug continued to shake me up and down. "We got a spy out here!"

Sanderson approached the window and peered out. "That would be Cooper. Bring him in here, Gus."

*I knew it.*

Gus drug me by my collar along the side of the building to the double doors and slung me around the corner. He waited for his boss to relieve me of my .32 and suit coat, then deposited me just shy of a comfortable pile of straw and threw my hat at me.

Sanderson put the gun in his pocket and then his hands on his knees. He looked down at me and shook his head from side to side. "Cooper, you are stickin' your nose where it don't belong."

I put on my hat, then reached to loosen my tie and gulp some dusty air. It smelled like ink.

"What are we goin' to do with him, boys?"

"Let's...." I wobbled myself to a standing position and ran a hand over the back of my neck. "Why not figure it this way? I'll catch my breath while your pals here clear a place off in the gravel. Then you and me can go about ten rounds."

Gus pointed towards the window. "Boss, there ain't no gravel—"

"Shad up!" Sanderson raised a backhand at the big thug but didn't follow through. "Sometimes I think your roof's got a leak."

He then pointed his finger at me. "I tell you what, Cooper. I'll figure it this way instead. There's a couple of jail cells over in the prison building, still intact. Station maintains 'em for old time's sake. In case they need to corner up a sick cow and keep an eye on it. They're about six foot deep, four foot wide, and not tall enough for you to stand and stretch your spine. You look sick to me. Why don't we put you in one of those?"

"It's that yellow bulb you got hanging there. The one the same color as *your* spine."

Sanderson grinned. "Now, you shouldn't have gone and said that, Cooper. I was just gonna put you in there for the night. But you've gone and insulted me. You've promoted yourself up from a life sentence to a death sentence. I'm gonna put you in there and let you rot!"

"Hey, boss." Gus took a step forward. From the look on the face of the guy running the printing press, the talking gorilla was about to say something he shouldn't.

"Boss, that ain't the plan. We ain't supposed ta—"

*Yep.*

The backhand made solid contact across beard stubble, and it sounded like sandpaper on knuckles.

"Am I gonna have to tie a can on your tail, Gus?"

The printing press guy's jaw dropped open like a two-dollar suitcase. A witness who could have stopped a car wreck but hesitated until it was too late.

Clueless, Gus rubbed his chin, and it made a scratchy noise. "WhatdaIsay?"

Sanderson turned to the press operator. "You! Get those finished and bundled. I want them ready to go by noon." To Gus the gorilla he said, "You, take Cooper here and toss him headfirst into one of those cells. Make sure it's one that locks. To me, he said, "The only thing on the menu is bread and water and we ain't got no bread and water."

I dropped my head and rushed at him like Jim Thorpe looking for the goal line. Unfortunately, their three-man defense converged on me and soon they had me trussed up like a Thanksgiving turkey ready for the fire. During the fracas my hat got kicked to the side and under the press.

This time, instead of dragging me by the collar, the gorilla and Sanderson knocked me down and grabbed the rope they'd tied around my ankles. The trip over to the old prison shredded the shirt on my back as they managed to navigate over every rock, brick threshold, and sharp stick they could spot.

The cell was as advertised. Not very deep, not very wide, and the curved ceiling made it not very tall. The floor was bare and cold, like a crypt. All in all the cell looked like half a brick cylinder with a gate on one end and a blank wall on the other. At least in the almost non-existent light I thought it was blank. Further inspection later would find a lot of scratches made by a lot of prisoners.

Sanderson knelt down and looked at me through the bars. "Funny time is over. I'd throw away the key, Cooper, but I think I'll hang on to it for a while."

Lying on my side with my ankles lashed together and my wrists tied in front of me, I stared back at him. "Why's that?"

"Now I'm going to tell you this in a friendly way. When you start to get really hungry and really thirsty I'm gonna come back and put it right here on the ground where you can see it. Just out of reach."

"I'm all tied up, you idiot! There ain't no way I'm going to be reaching for anything."

He shook his head from side to side. "You're a resourceful man, Cooper. I have no doubt you'll be out of those ropes in a couple of hours."

Trying to see him without rolling over on my raw back, I gave him my best 'Don't make me come out there' look. "What's your game, Sanderson?"

"No game."

"Why'd you punch Mary in the face?"

"It got in my way."

"To quote one of your earlier remarks, 'You shouldn't have gone and said that.'"

"I've got work to do, Cooper. You're not worth any more of my time." He motioned to the gorilla. "Let's go, Gus."

"We gonna just leave him here?"

"There won't be anyone around until Monday.

By then if the cold don't get him, the rats will."

"But boss, somebody's gonna come check on those cows and —"

"Then go in there and gag him!" Sanderson had that look someone has when the other someone thinks of something they didn't. He sure didn't like being made to look stupid in front of his prisoner.

And right now, he looked pretty stupid, and I made sure my expression conveyed to him I thought so.

Gus disappeared out the door while Sanderson fumed, and I snickered.

"Shut up, Cooper! I oughta have him shove it all the way down your throat!"

Gus reappeared with a big blue bandanna and my coat, took the key from Sanderson, unlocked the cell door while his boss held my own gun on me, and commenced to tie a knot in it and force said knot between my teeth. The coat he tossed to the back.

Of course, I was uncooperative.

"Tie it real tight, Gus!" Sanderson slammed the bars shut after the gorilla crawled out. "Get back to the press. See if he's ready to load up some bundles." Brandishing my gun, he knelt once more and spit through the bars. "I really don't like you, Cooper."

Beyond him, in the shadows, a silhouette moved to the right and by the combined sound of a body bouncing off a sheet of tin and some choice words aimed at said tin, I gathered whoever it was had tripped and fell.

Sanderson turned on his heels and then up and ran toward the shadows. The fact he didn't yell condescending remarks told me the faller wasn't Gus. "You, okay?" He reached out and disappeared into the darkness. "What are you doing here?"

"I've cut my hand!"

The low voice might have been male or female. I was fairly sure I'd know it if I heard it again.

"Get me up from here. Find some water and a towel."

With that, the voices withdrew as tin rattled and the pair left the barn.

At this point I realized Sanderson still had my .32. A Harrington & Richardson American Double Action my father had given me when he retired from the police force. It was going to be beyond a pleasure to get that bean shooter back.

With the side of my face on the ground, first order of business was to work over to my suit coat for a pillow. Then I thought about my raincoat. I'd left it on the train.

# FIVE

The rest of the night proved to not be up to my usual standards. I preferred a soft mattress. Full of goose feathers plucked from geese raised by fair maidens. My pillow the same. Sheets made with something other than straw. The first aromas of the morning, coffee and bacon.

Currently.... If they bottled it as a cologne, it'd be labeled "Old Barn" for the man who wants to smell like livestock and repel the ladies.

From my vantage point on the cell floor, I eyed two things. A window very high up the wall, with morning sunlight filtering through the "Old Barn" infused air, and a strange cage made of thin metal strappings. Its design appeared to be more likely to keep someone out, than in.

Since I had a lot of time to stare at it, I contemplated all of the possible uses it might have had in this converted prison and settled on guard watch post.

Which I found out later was entirely correct.

Satisfied with that, I contemplated for a while who the person was who fell into the tin sheets. Familiar voice, but the tone was different.

Eventually I shook that from my brain and set out to work on an escape plan. You can do a lot of working on your escape plan when you're all gagged and tied up like a Christmas goose.

Now, I'm not giving away the farm here in letting you know I eventually escaped. How else can I be relating this tale? But, since I wasn't an eyewitness to how it came about, at least not to all of it, I'll bring this story up to speed by piecing together what I was told by my employer, Arcadia Vyne, his secretary Rodrick, and his chauffeur, a short stocky lad named Baylee.

Young Baylee can't seem to tell you anything without starting out with what he had for breakfast, so that seems the best place to go back to.

Before Mary caught Sanderson's fist in the face.

Before the lineup.

Before my unfortunate incarceration in Wyoming's finest Prison Resort.

I will however interject that I did have four visitors who were absolutely no help in springing me, or so I thought at the time.

A wolf and three young boys.

The boys stormed in first. The shortest, but I think the oldest, of the trio spotted me as he ran by. They were kicking an old rusty can through the big building and I heard it long before I saw him.

When he set eyes on me, trussed up and gagged, he skidded to a stop, squatted in front of the cell door, and stared at me with a hard stare like a kid who'd found a frog in a mud puddle and couldn't decide if his sister needed a joke played on her.

I gurgled and sputtered, but he didn't seem to understand gurgle and sput.

Soon his chums came along in a cloud of straw dust, wondering why he'd not returned with the can, and they too skidded, squatted, and stared. Sometimes at me and sometimes at each other. They never said a word between them. They did like to point at me a lot. And scratch their heads.

This went on for a good ten minutes, or as best I

could tell without being able to see my watch.

Then the wolf arrived.

The big bad wolf and the three little boys.

No huffing. No puffing. A snarl sufficed and they hightailed it out of there like their pants were on fire.

I quickly discovered the wolf also did not understand gurgle and sput.

But, I digress.

Here's what I learned from Baylee's report of Saturday morning last. Even though I occupied a seat at the breakfast table for most of it, he felt compelled to start at the beginning and tell it as if he observed it through the eyes of a bug on the wall.

Yeah, as I've said, I've given away the fact I got out of there alive.

You obviously read crime novels.

So, we'll say no more about it.

# Six

Seven o'clock the previous Saturday morning.

Arcadia Vyne sat at the head of the long table, as he did every morning, and pushed eggs and sausage onto his fork with the flat edge of a knife. He liked his eggs poached and his sausage —

[This is where I interrupted, "Get on with it, Baylee Boy. We don't need the menu."]

Vyne at the head of the table, Cooper – you - to his right. Mr. Rodrick, and me, farther down after we'd been silently served by Stewart and he'd taken his place across the way.

Better? Okay.

You teetered on the back two legs of your chair with a cup of coffee in one hand and the folded *Rocky Mountain News* in the other. A write up on the obit page made you laugh. "Hah, Ha! Now what are the odds?"

"Fifty-fifty," answered Arcadia Vyne.

"What?" You lowered the paper.

"All odds are fifty-fifty," Arcadia Vyne nodded and took a sip of orange juice. "Fifty-fifty."

"What are you talking about, Professor?" He doesn't like you to call him that you know.

So, the Prof — Arcadia Vyne says, "Fifty-fifty. Either things happen or they don't. There are no other options. It can't almost happen, because if it could almost but not actually, it did not happen. It cannot almost not happen, because if that were the case, it did."

You sat your coffee cup on the table, then on the saucer after Stewart gave you the eye. "Obit in the *Rocky* here says nobody died yesterday. You're sayin' it's a fifty-fifty chance that either somebody died, or nobody died?"

"Yes, that is what I'm saying." He took another sip of his juice and nodded slightly.

"I'm not buyin' it."

"No?"

"No."

You leaned in toward him and held out your hand, palm up. "Even if the population of Denver is, what? Couple of hundred thousand people?"

"The 1930 census recorded 287,861."

Well, you can't argue that man didn't have a brain like a steel elephant.

"Okay, 280,000 and change," you said.

You, on the other hand, Mr. Cooper, sometimes like to live in the gray area of things. Anyway, then you said, "So, if nobody died wouldn't the odds be all that to one?"

"No, Jonas."

"My old maid fifth-grade math teacher would not agree."

Mr. Rodrick held his napkin to his face to hide his laugh. I saw it 'cause I was sittin' right next to him.

"Okay, Professor. How 'bout this one?" you asked. "Somebody did die yesterday, but it was nobody." You leaned back in your chair and grinned. "Or let's say it another way. Maybe nobody did die. Then there are no obits in this paper. I would think those odds would be astronomical. The stars would be lining up all in a nice row between the sun and the Moon. As a matter of fact, I think I'll go outside and see." You started to push your chair back.

"It's daylight, my boy. No stars."

"But they're lined up out there. Even if you can't see them. Have to be. No obits in the *Rocky* today. Never happened before. Will never happen again."

"What will never happen again?"

"A day where nobody dies."

"You just said he did."

"Yeah. So?"

"If he died today, yesterday more likely if it's in this morning's paper, but if he died today, then you would in fact be correct in your statement it will never happen again. A man can physically die only once." He paused. "Of course, we're talking about the present day. Not of those mentioned in the Bible."

Everybody knows Arcadia Vyne knows his Scriptures and loves to play games. He'd bought into yours and he had our heads spinning like a whirling dervish. My head hurt thinking this one over and I could tell yours was too.

Stewart was starin' up at the ceiling. Sometimes he does that when he's workin' on a problem. "Mr. Cooper you say there are no obits in that paper?"

"Did I?" you replied.

"I think.... No.... Somebody did die, but just one.

Or nobody died."

"Yes."

"For goodness sakes...."

Vyne put a slender finger to the side of his cheek. "This reminds me of a man I once had the pleasure seeing in a British music hall while on a sales expedition in '31. This comedian, I believe Will Hay was his name. He performed a routine where he pretended to be a schoolmaster interviewing a schoolboy named Howe. The lad came from a hamlet called Ware, but he had moved to Wye."

"What?" you asked.

"Wye."

Stewart chuckled. "I seem to recall it as well, sir. There was something similar with a baseball theme on *The Kate Smith Hour* radio program a few months back. Those two young comedians had everyone in stitches."

I don't think I'd ever heard Stewart talk as much. Plus, I don't think I had ever seen Stewart smile before. At least not big enough to see he had a good full set of teeth.

You scratched the top of your head and leaned back in your chair again. "Schoolmasters? Baseball? Kate Smith? Let's get to my original question for the Professor."

Vyne nodded and finished the last of the breakfast on his plate. He calmly lowered his fork to the table with one hand and lifted the cloth napkin from his lap to dab the corners of his mouth with the other. "Jonas, you stated, 'Somebody did die yesterday, but it was nobody.'"

"Yes, I stated that statement. What say you to it?"

He slowly lowered the napkin back to his lap and turned his thin neck so he could arch his eyebrows at you. "I'm quite sad to hear this, Jonas. He'd been a dear friend for a very long time. One of the first merchants in the area to stock Vyne Tea. How did he decease?"

The look on your face was priceless. Wished I'd had my Brownie handy to get a snap of it. Utter shock.

"How'd you know?" You pointed at Stewart. "He handed me this paper the moment after he entered the room. He had it in his hand." You lifted the paper and studied the folds in the light from above like you thought they were see-through. "Every morning. Same thing. Stewart enters. Hands me the paper. I read the sports and funnies and obits while you eat. Since the day I set foot in this place, Professor, you have never read the paper before me." You looked at me and arched your brow. "Baylee, you told him!"

"Not, me!" I shot back.

"Stewart!"

"No, Mr. Cooper. I've been in the presence of Mr. Vyne just long enough to serve his breakfast. Then back to the kitchen for ours, then the paper to you."

You looked fit to be tied and dropped the paper on the floor. "How'd you do it, Professor? You don't come out of your room till the bacon sizzle wafts up to the second floor."

"There are other ways a man can receive information."

You looked about. "The phone didn't ring. No doorbell this morning." You slapped your knee. "I got it! Carrier pigeon. A bird with a message tied to its leg flew in your window this morning and landed on your pillow. Pecked you on the ear. Fanned you with its wings until you sat upright and removed said message from said bird's said leg."

Vyne's expression held.

You were halfway out of your chair. "Well?"

"If I told you, how can I expect you to learn to deduce properly?"

"I can deduce properly just fine, thank you."

He held out an open palm and gestured you back into your chair. "You have some skill. It can be better. Think on this today and you'll figure it out."

Curiosity was getting the best of me by this time. "Come on, Cooper," I said. "Read the obit. Who died? Or who didn't?"

Mr. Rodrick nodded his two cents worth.

"Oh, all right," you said.

Then you fetched the paper off the floor with a wide sweep of your arm without ever leaving the chair and aired out the pages in front of you. "Okay, let's see now." With a lick of your thumb, you worked your way to the section and read:

"Norbert Olympus Bodie, known to friends and family as N. O., passed from this life in the presence of his grandniece, Millicent Bodie Mundene, and his staff of caretakers and house servants."

"Ah!" Mr. Rodrick and I said at the same time.

"N. O. Bodie," I added.

"Yes, N. O. Bodie," you repeated. "A businessman in the Denver area since before the turn of the century. A landowner, merchant, member of numerous boards of directors, and philanthropist, his holdings employ hundreds of Denver's fine citizens.

"Bodie, the last of his line, arrived in Denver by train from St. Louis with no more than the clothes on his back and $10,000 in his pocket."

You whistled.

"The Bodie family had made its fortune in speculation and real estate in North Carolina. His roots go back to Bodie Island, originally known as Bodie's Island or Body Island which formed in 1738 when an inlet opened up separating the island from Hatteras Island. Some speculate Bodie Island received that name because of numerous shipwrecks in the Outer Banks, however N. O. Bodie's ancestor, Robert Boddy (or perhaps Boddie) came to America from England on the HMS *Safety* in the early 1600s and it was his descendants who settled the area.

"Services for Mr. Bodie will be held Tuesday evening at six o'clock on the first floor of the Mining Exchange. As many know, Bodie maintained his offices on the sixth floor of the Exchange. Interment will be later in Bodie, California, an old mining town near the Nevada state line where he had staked his first claim."

You lowered the paper and peered over the top at the Professor. "So, you knew this guy?"

"For many years."

"He sold your tea."

"Yes, one of the first to do so."

"Here in Denver."

"Yes, and all over the world."

"That so?" You pursed your lips. "How'd you know he died."

The Professor shook his head. "As I said, you will have to figure that out for yourself. Now, are you finished with what is left of the newspaper? I'd like to check the weather forecast."

"Sure, here." You folded it up and placed it on the corner of the table. "Well, I got nothin' up for the rest of the day. All day to think. Think and think some more. Think about you and no body."

"Enjoy yourself. But remember you four have chess practice after lunch." The Professor nodded to Stewart as he removed his plate and refreshed his cup of tea.

You stood and brushed the side of your pants leg. "I'll do that. I'll practice my chess game, just so someday I can brag I crowned your king."

"That's checkers young man."

"Oh, I'm so gonna enjoy myself."

I could tell you were irritated. You get this look on your face. It's like the folds on your forehead are trying to reach down and touch your chin. Your eyes get all squinty and....

[This is where I told him, "I get the point, Baylee."]

So, you said, "I've got most of the day before my

date with Mary Smith this evening. See you later. I'm going to spend the day in my booth at Pug's and drink pots of coffee." With that, you grabbed your hat and headed out the door.

["I know what I did. And I never did figure out...."]

Oh, you will when you hear what happened after you left and the doorbell rang. Mr. Rodrick's gotta tell this part. I wasn't there.

# Seven

They stood on the porch [related Rick, as I call him, in his best British voice which I'll not try to mimic here] and he produced a card of introduction as if he had never been here before. Of which of course they had, as you know, because they are our next-door neighbors.

They being Mr. and Mrs. Cuthbert Preston III. Third generation old money. Owner of the four largest dry good warehouses in town and controlling stock in a local bank, two mines, and significant holdings in six or more others. One thing they both held in common with Mr. Vyne, aside from living on the same street, were large holdings of stocks and seats on the Board of Directors for the Mustang Gap Mining Company.

She, being his wife, Evangelina, was dressed to the nines with full makeup and pearls. The grandfather clock in the hallway chimed nine o'clock in the morning. After all, one simply didn't go out in public without putting on the airs, even if 'public' meant down the sidewalk to the next mansion on the block. Her perfume smelled of roses and mothballs. The one thing lacking – shoes. She wiggled her macerated barefooted toes on the cool stone and clasped her ring-covered fingers below her heavily rouged right cheek.

Mr. Preston lacked even more of his attire, namely pants. His upper torso consisted of dress coat, vest, club tie with tie bar, a sharply creased handkerchief in his upper pocket, a watch on a chain, a monocle, and a bowler hat. Below the belt, stripped blue pajamas and Italian slippers. Near his left heel, the eager eyes of Dauphine, their small Pomeranian, peered up as if anticipating a treat.

I'll also note that I very seldom ever witnessed Mr. Preston with his hands outside his pockets. Even with the pajama bottoms, his hands were buried inside the pockets with the little dog's leash snaking out the left one.

They looked quite the trio as she edged five-foot ten in her bare feet and the top of his bowler leveled with her shoulders.

As they say in the Sunday comic section, a real Mutt and Jeff. She being Mutt and he being Milquetoast.

"We'd appreciate seeing Mr. Vyne." Her voice at a decent level carried the baritone of an opera singer.

Her husband nodded and released the card of introduction into my care. Now that I mention it, he did have his right hand out of his pocket. He had on a thin brown leather glove.

"I'm afraid, Mr. and Mrs. Preston," I responded in my way without looking at the card, "Mr. Vyne has ascended to his room to read. After that, as usual, he will spend his Saturday afternoon in his laboratory and won't want to be disturbed until after five."

"I see." She glanced over and down at her husband. "Perhaps the nice Mr. Cooper?"

The Pomeranian barked.

Mrs. Preston smiled. "Dauphine took such a liking to Mr. Cooper when he found her and brought her home to us."

"Yes, ma'am."

She leaned to peer beyond into the entryway. "Is he available for consultation?"

"No, I'm afraid Mr. Cooper has departed for the day. We don't expect him back till late."

"Oh, dear," Mr. Preston spoke at last. His voice a perfect match to his stature. Small and weak.

"Being a private detective, it's not uncommon," I assured them.

"I see, perhaps —"

"Perhaps then, you might make an exception and query Arcadia?" Mrs. Preston nudged her husband's slipper with the side of her pruney bare foot. "It's very important."

"May, I inquire as to the nature of your visit?"

"Well, you see —"

"It's our daughter, Rowena," blurted out Mr. Preston. "She's been kidnapped!"

I conveyed to them how disturbing this news was.

"You'll have to excuse my husband, he's jumpy when he hasn't had his tonic."

"Mr. Vyne will certainly want to speak with you," I told them. "Please step in." With this, I escorted them to the drawing room. "Please make yourselves comfortable. I'm sure he will receive you shortly. I then turned on my heels, walked to the stairs, and ascended.

Mr. Vyne, as per his routine, would sit in his favorite chair on his landing above the garden and read a book. Most decidedly earlier than usual, my three crisp raps brought him immediately to see why I had arrived sooner than expected.

"Yes, Rodrick?"

"Mr. and Mrs. Preston to see you, Boss." I presented the card.

"At this hour? With card?" He retrieved his half-moon reading glasses from the top of his head. "What's going on?" He opened the door wide and cinched his morning robe tight about his thin waist. "They never venture out beyond their property line before noon. What's the matter?"

"They say their daughter has been kidnapped, sir."

"Rowena? Kidnapped? Why I was just taking to Cuthbert from my balcony yesterday morning." He pointed in that direction. "He told me about N. O. passing but said nothing about Rowena."

[Blast, that's how he knew.]

"Most certainly." I said to him, "I gather it is a recent dilemma, sir."

"All right, Rodrick. Send Stewart up. Tell them

I'll be down in a few minutes. See if they've had breakfast."

"Yes, sir." I nodded and stepped away from his door. When it shut, I turned and descended the stairs, relayed the summons to Stewart, and then returned to the drawing room.

Dauphine sat in Mr. Vyne's chair.

Mrs. Preston filled the right end of the divan.

Mr. Preston paced in front of the fireplace. I believe if it had held a fire, he would have fanned the flames.

"Well?" Mrs. Preston held her arms out. "Will he see us?"

"Yes, madam. He will be down in a few moments. He inquired if you had need of breakfast."

Dauphine barked. Not at the mention of a meal, but at the sight of Caffeine. The cat had appeared on the back of the divan, preening her black face with a paw as if she had no use for any of us.

I drew the two Prestons' gaze back from Caffeine to me with, "Madam? Sir? Breakfast?"

Mr. Preston shrugged and pocketed his monocle. "I don't think I can eat at a time like this."

It was at that moment I realized I had forgotten to take his hat at the door. Not daring to let Mr. Vyne become aware of this, I tried to step in time with the little man, but he moved too fast for me. He was so preoccupied with their dilemma, I didn't think he would notice, so I snatched the bowler from his head and held it behind me. His hair was decidedly parted down the middle.

The hat wiggled in my fingers. So, I turned to find Caffeine who had hopped to a chair back to rub against it. Before I could shoo her away, Mr. Vyne entered the room with Stewart just behind.

The boss had changed into one of his more dapper suits, the one with the blue cravat and matching handkerchief. His reading glasses now hung on his chest by a chain from his neck. With just a few strides he was in front of Mrs. Preston on the divan peering down at her bare feet.

"Evangeline, can I have Stewart fetch you a pair of slippers?"

She held her legs out straight, the soles of her feet almost touching Mr. Vyne's knees. "Oh, my! I'm half dressed! Oh, Arcadia! She raised her hands into the air as if surrendering. Her legs still outstretched. "What are we to do? What are *we* to do? Our Rowena.... Gone."

Mr. Preston stopped pacing and stepped toward Mr. Vyne. "Yes, Arcadia. Gone." He shivered.

"Stewart."

"Yes, sir."

"Bring Mrs. Preston a pair of your slippers."

I anticipated this as her feet were larger than the boss's and most certainly almost as big as Stewart's.

"Rodrick, light the fire," he continued. "A log or two more when you do."

"Yes, sir."

"Thank you, Rodrick."

"Yes, sir." As I stepped back to make my exit, Mrs. Preston pointed at her husband. "Cuthbert, take one of your nerve pills."

"I can't, Dearest." He pursed his lips. "They're in my other pajamas."

❦

When I returned with the wood, Stewart had just handed Mrs. Preston a pair of his slippers.

I added the logs and lit the fire. The boss sat on the divan next to Mrs. Preston. Mr. Preston had settled into the tall wingback caddy corner to them. He continued to tremble.

The shoes on Mrs. Preston's feet were just a fit - barely.

The lighting of the logs in the fireplace transpired as they discussed the disappearance of the young lady. A plain simple girl in my opinion from the times she had visited with her parents at one of Mr. Vyne's game parties or social events. She stood taller than her mother. A whole lot taller than her father. Always had her hair tied up into a tight bun on the back of her head. Dressed smartly. Wore silver rimmed glasses which made her look intelligent. Well educated. Decidedly single. And very, very shy.

"When did this happen?" the boss asked as he patted Mrs. Preston's hand.

"We don't know for sure."

"When did you see her last?"

"In the evening. At dinner," volunteered Mr. Preston. "Irish spiced beef and baked apple pudding. Two of her favorites."

This brought a loud sobbing sound from Mrs. Preston. "I had forgotten. Yes, two of her favorites."

"Did she seem all right at dinner?" asked the boss.

"Oh, most assuredly." Another sob and before he knew it, she snatched the matching blue handkerchief out of his jacket pocket.

"You had coffee afterward?"

"Of course."

"And I smoked a cigar," said Mr. Preston.

The boss glanced at him for a moment and then

returned his inquisition back to Madam.

"Has she been seeing anyone?"

"Arcadia!"

"Now, Evangeline, the girl is almost thirty. You have to admit it is a possibility she has found a beau and may have gone off with him."

"She wouldn't." Her eyes went to her husband. "Would she? Cuthbert. Oh, would she?"

"I think not." He shook his head.

"I agree. She's shown no indication.... She spends her time with her books. I don't think there's a man out there who measures up to any Prince Charming she's read about."

The boss nodded his agreement.

I did as well and reached for a poker to coax the fire.

"Did you see her retire to her room?"

"Cuthbert?"

"Yes, Dearest. She said 'good night, father' on the way up the stairs. Clara followed behind her with a glass of warm milk."

It was at this time that Baylee waved his chauffeur's cap at me from the kitchen door and made a pantomime of someone bearing a plate of food and a fork. I gave him a quick head motion to go away. With that he shrugged, gave me a wave of dismissal, and retreated back into the kitchen.

"Evangeline," said the boss. "What happened this morning?"

"Clara came to me in the garden and said Rowena was not answering her door."

"Was that common?"

"Oh, no. Rowena never sleeps in. She had mentioned at dinner her desire to help me in the garden."

"What did you do after Clara told you this?"

"I called for Cuthbert."

"Yes, she called for me."

"And you both went up to check on her?"

"No, Dearest asked me to go, and I did."

"You went and knocked."

"Yes, I went and knocked."

"No answer."

"No answer. How did you know?"

The boss ignored that. "Did you enter her room?"

"Of course, I did not."

"Why not?"

"Why... Why... She might not have been decent. No, I called for Clara to go in."

"Not decent! Cuthbert, you didn't tell me that." Mrs. Preston glared at him. I would never want to be on the receiving end of a deadly glare like that.

"I'm sorry, Dearest." He looked to have physically collapsed down into his clothes. There he sat in that chair, all coat and very little man.

The boss pointed at him. "Continue, Cuthbert. What happened when Clara went in?"

The shrinking man reversed course and began to grow in his collar like a turtle coming out of its shell. "I heard her call. 'Rowena,' softly at first, but more forcefully and as she toured the room."

"You could see her do this from the door?"

"Yes, from the door."

"Did you ever enter the room?"

"Yes. Clara looked at me and shrugged her shoulders. I went in and stood in the middle of the room. From there I directed her to check the closest, the armoire, under the bed, and the private bath."

"Were any of Rowena's clothes missing?"

"Clara didn't seem to think so."

"Her toiletries?"

"We didn't think to check."

"Then what did you do?"

"Well, of course, we explored the rest of the house. Clara went through all the upstairs rooms. Dearest went to the kitchen. I headed for the garage and storage."

"I don't recall that you have a driver, do you?"

"Oh, no." This from Mrs. Preston. "We always call a taxi."

"No one else in the house besides you, Cuthbert, and Clara?"

"Cook was in the kitchen. She hadn't seen Rowena either."

"Curious." The boss clasped his hands as he did when he worked a problem. "What did the police have to say?"

The pair turned to look at each other.

Eventually Mrs. Preston took a deep breath and bellowed, "Police? We never called them!"

The boss appeared taken aback. "You haven't called the police? Why not?"

"I don't think it ever crossed my mind. Cuthbert?"

"No, hadn't crossed my mind. That is until now. Now that you've mentioned it."

"You think Rowena's been kidnapped and you never thought to call the police?"

Mrs. Preston gulped air. "No."

I held up a finger. "Might I ask a question, sir?"

"Of course, Rodrick. Your input is appreciated. What do you want to ask?"

"Well, sir. Mr. and Mrs. Preston. I'm wondering

what makes you suspect kidnapping?"

"Isn't it obvious?" Mr. Preston looked at me like he didn't appreciate my input. Servants are to be seen and not heard and all that.

"It's a valid question, Cuthbert," the boss said, nodding his approval my way. "Just because she isn't in the house, why would you think she had been kidnapped? She might have gone out for a walk. She might have discovered she had a library book overdue. There are a hundred reasons besides kidnapping to explain why she isn't in the house."

Dauphine, who had been sleeping in the boss's chair barked as Mr. Preston's hand came out of his pajama pocket with the end of the leash and a piece of paper.

I amend myself. Apparently he had on just one glove.

He held the paper up for all to see. "Why this ransom note, of course."

# EIGHT

**R**odrick continued with what happened Saturday morning.

The boss sent the Prestons home with instructions to call the police. We didn't see them for the rest of the day but did observe the coming and going of a police vehicle.

With that out of our hands, the boss recruited me down to his laboratory to sample some new teas.

❦

No additional information came our way until Sunday morning.

[In case you've forgotten, by this time, I was trussed up like a Christmas goose in the former Wyoming Territorial Prison slash Agricultural Experiment Station.]

We sat in our usual pew at church, Baylee, myself, and the boss. Despite your absence at breakfast, we expected to see you there. But your usual spot, hugging the end of the pew near the windows, remained empty when the service began.

You know how the acoustics are in that old building and while we were in the third chorus of the first hymn, the double doors creaked open at the rear of the room, and we heard the sound over our singing. Even though we often have visitors, the times are plainly posted outside, and I can't remember the last instance someone came into the service during the middle of a song. Usually, they stand outside and wait. Of, course we kept singing, *Worthy Art Thou*, and the song leader, who could see what we couldn't, tacked on a repeat of the first verse.

Before the next hymn, the leader behind the lectern asked us to stand, which we did with hymnals raised and this is when a shortish man, hat in hand, sidestepped into your vacant spot on the pew. Not that the spot belonged to you, but in a sense that it was where you sat more often than not. He whispered something to the boss and the boss shushed him and fell in with the next song. It was then I realized it was Detective Raft.

Red-faced, he shuffled his feet and grabbed a hymnal from the back of the pew, opened it to a random page, and tried to mouth the words.

I held my book up high in front of my face so I could turn my head and see what he was doing. He swiveled his head on his neck to the left and to the right. I could tell he was trying to figure out why we were singing without a piano or an organ. He grunted.

A petite lady in front of him turned and made eye contact. She held an index finger to her lips.

When the song ended and a few 'Amens!' responded from various points, we sat.

As the preacher switched places with the song leader, Raft whispered some more. I couldn't make out what he said, but I did hear the boss whisper back, "No, I haven't seen Mr. Cooper. He didn't return last evening. Nor at breakfast."

Raft spoke a bit louder, "So, you don't know he got slugged and his date went to the hospital?"

This perked the attention of the row of people both in front and behind us.

The petite lady turned again and frowned.

He frowned back at her.

I have to say she didn't care for that at all.

"This can wait until we're outside." The boss slipped his reading glasses from his nose and let them hang by the chain.

"Suit yourself." Raft shrugged and put the song-book back in its place. He then made an attempt to stand but the boss, stronger than he looks, took hold of his elbow and parked him in place. "You're here. Now stay. You might learn something new."

Detective Raft craned his head to look toward the back of the room. The row in front of us and the row behind us did the same.

I had to swivel completely around to see what they all saw, Sergeant Griz Asher looking like a dog who just wandered into a room full of cats. Uncomfortable and searching for an exit. I know I shouldn't be judging someone in church. Just reporting what I saw.

The big policeman fumbled a step back into the double doors but stopped when Raft contorted his body about and pointed at a back pew.

Griz Asher shrugged his shoulders sheepishly. Well, as sheepishly as a man his size can. Then he awkwardly slid into a pew on his left.

The preacher cleared his throat.

Everyone returned their attention forward.

Detective Raft huffed.

The petite lady drew in her shoulders.

"It is certainly nice to see we have guests this morning." He gestured toward Raft and then in the direction of Asher in the back. "Welcome."

Raft nodded weakly and I'm not sure what the sergeant did.

The sermon for the morning was from *Luke 15:11-32* about the prodigal son. Detective Raft was somewhat attentive, and I believe it may have been Sergeant Asher I heard snoring in the back.

When it came time to take communion the detective looked bewildered but partook anyway, trying to mimic what he saw others do. The collection plate was another matter and he passed it along like it held fire and brimstone.

More singing and at the last 'Amen' Raft, who'd been sweating for a while, stood and moved down the outer aisle with a gait worthy of a man twice his height.

I stood in time to see him slap his sergeant over the head with his hat and exit out the double doors.

Sergeant Asher stood slowly, raised his arms over his head to help a yawn, and then followed.

We found Raft under a Yellowwood tree, fanning himself with his fedora. The sergeant stood a few feet away, leaning against a car door.

The boss offered his hand to the detective. "Thank you for being our guest this morning."

"Falderal," returned Raft with no hand to shake.

"Now, what's this about our man Jonas?"

"I tried to tell you in there. He got clocked on the head."

"Is he okay?"

"Walking upright the last time I saw him."

"And Mary Smith?"

"Crumb busted her jaw good," volunteered the sergeant. "She's gonna be in that hospital for a while."

"Did you arrest anyone?"

Raft put on his hat and adjusted it till he was satisfied. "We brought a guy in, Sanderson. Had him dead to rights and your Cooper refused to peg him in the lineup. He knew who was who. On top of it, he was sore about his date getting messed up."

"Why would he not identify him?"

"Beats me. Jonas Cooper's missing a fender. All he had to do was give the word and we'd have had Sanderson off the street. Been wanting him as a guest since he rolled into town. Cooper let him go, free as air."

"This was late last night?"

"More like early this morning."

"You saw him leave the police station?"

Raft tamped his foot in the grass and the more his irritation rose, the more acerbic his voice became. "Not exactly. I just saw Cooper leave the lineup room. Don't know where he went after that. Just assumed he left."

"Before or after Sanderson?"

"Again. Don't know." The detective pulled his pipe out of his coat pocket and stuck it in his mouth. "He just vanished."

Baylee, Stewart, and I had been watching this tennis match of a conversation go on from nearby.

The boss reached out and put his hand on Raft's arm. "Then why are you here looking for Jonas?"

"Considered Cooper might be here with you. I have other questions to ask him. The more I thought about what he did the fishier it smelled."

"Have you checked the hospital? Doctor's offices?"

"We checked the vet!" Asher barked from over at the car.

"That's enough of that, Sergeant," Raft yelled

back. "It's time for us to go."

The boss held onto the Raft's arm. "Was Jonas badly injured?"

"Had a knot on his head a show dog could jump over. But he's got a thick skull. He seemed all right."

"Could he have been in shock, perhaps? Walked away and blacked out somewhere?"

"Now, why didn't I think of that?" Sarcasm dripped from the statement as Raft pulled his arm free. "Your man has wandered off. Not my day to raise him." He brushed his sleeve. "You see him. You tell him to come see me." He took the pipe out of his mouth and poked the boss in the chest with the stem. "Today." With that, he buttoned his coat and walked away.

We all stepped forward and huddled about the boss.

"What do you suppose that's all about?" Baylee looked past me toward the street. "He doesn't like Cooper."

"I know," replied the boss. "For him to come here, and sit through half a worship service no less, he desperately wants to know where Jonas is."

All this while the other members of the congregation were filing out and heading in different directions. The preacher came by and asked if everything was all right.

The boss simply replied, "We hope so."

With a, "Let me know if there is anything I can do," the preacher shook our hands and moved on to another group.

"Do? That's a good question." Baylee fished the car key from his pocket. "What are we going to do, sir?"

"Baylee, you and I are going to go to the police station and see if we can ascertain where Jonas went after he left there."

"And me, sir?" I asked.

Rodrick I want you to go to the hospital and check on Mary Smith. See if she can shed any light on what is going on."

# Nine

Rodrick's visit to the hospital proved unproductive as he reported he found Mary Smith asleep with her jaw wired shut.

We didn't have idea one where you'd gone off to, Cooper. What with the Prestons' daughter, Rowena, missing as well, it appeared to be a regular epidemic. The Profess.... See you got me callin' him that now!

[It's okay, Baylee. I won't tell. Go ahead if it's any easier.]

We were all worried. Well, Detective Raft, didn't seem worried or that big Griz... anyway, after church the Professor had me drive him down to the police station on Larimer. He went and stood on the main steps for a really long time. First he looked up the street. Then he looked down the street. Then across. After that went on for a while, he'd have me go way down to the corner and walk around or go stand behind a lamppost, or duck into the fire station. Boy, he wore me out.

Eventually he decided you had gone toward 15th. Off he started to walk until he waved for me to get in the car and follow along. Down to 17th he went, looking up at the buildings along the way.

Then around the corner we went, heading west.

Arriving at Union Station, he sat his little self on a bench and watched freight trains go by for a while. Every so often he'd stand and look up the tracks and down the tracks.

"Baylee," the Professor said. "Go over to the ticket window and retrieve a train schedule."

"Yes, sir." A couple of minutes later I had placed it in his hand, and he had perched his reading glasses on his nose.

For fifteen minutes, I timed him, he read the thing cover to cover. Front to back. Every so often, he pulled out his pocket watch and talked to it, or at least that's what it looked like to me. I guess he was just doin' some figurin'.

"Baylee," he said. "Go over to the ticket window and ask if he knows who worked the last night shift."

"Yes, sir." A couple of minutes later I told him it was a man named Willoughby."

"Will he be working tonight?"

"Uh, I didn't ask."

"Go ask."

"Yes, sir." Off to the window I went, asked, and returned to the bench. He was gone. "What now?" I said out loud. "Is everybody gonna up and disappear?"

Mr. Vyne.... The Professor tapped me on the shoulder. I tried to jump out of my skin and nearly ended up on the tracks.

"What did you find out, Baylee?"

I pulled off my cap and wiped sweat from my forehead with the back of my hand. "The agent, Willoughby, will be here tonight. Shift starts at six."

"We have a bit of time." He consulted his watch at the end of its chain. "Let's go to the park."

"No disrespect, sir, but what with Cooper missing and the neighbor's daughter and all, what are we going to find at the park?"

"Geese."

✹❧☙

I had no idea the Professor could be entertained by a bunch of waddling birds, but that's exactly how we passed the rest of Sunday afternoon waiting for that station man to get to work. I spent most of my time skipping rocks on the lake. One was a seven hopper. You shoulda seen it…. Uh, but about ten to six we headed back to the car and got to the station just as a young man with a poor excuse for a mustache sat down behind the ticket window.

"You are Mr. Willoughby?" asked the Professor.

The young agent licked his bottom lip.

"That's me. How'd you know my name?"

"We inquired. My name is Arcadia Vyne. May I ask you a few questions?"

Willoughby looked past us, and I glanced back to see what he was looking at. Nothing.

"Maybe. If a line piles up behind you, you'll have to buy a ticket or get out of the way."

"Fair enough." The Professor reached into his coat and pulled out a long thin wallet. From this he pulled out a two-dollar bill.

"Hey, mister, I don't take play money."

"I suppose you don't see these very often, Mr. Willoughby. If you can help me with my inquiries about my associate, it's yours."

"It's real? Spendable money?"

"If you'd rather not have...."

"I didn't say that. What'd you want to know?"

"Last night, after sunset, two men bought tickets."

"I sell a lot of tickets."

The Professor then described you to a tee. The way he painted that word picture, it could have been your brother.

Willoughby thought for a moment, then nodded. "I seem to remember a guy like that."

"And the other man? Just before?"

"Yeah. Two guys."

"Did they both buy tickets?"

"They did."

"Where to?"

The young man smoothed his excuse for a mustache and pushed his cap back on his head. "I'm not sure if I'm supposed to say. You a cop?"

"No, the man I described works for me. I'd like to know where he's gone."

"You checkin' up on him? What'd he do, run off with the till?" The snicker came out from behind the mustache as a kind of snort. "Now you mention it, he did look kind of shifty."

[He said that? Shifty?]

"The first man or second?" asked the Professor.

A look of confusion crossed the young clerk's face. He removed his cap and scratched the back of his head. "I guess the guy with the loud tie looked a little less trustworthy than the second."

The Professor slid the bill forward.

With eyes on his prize, the clerk pulled his hat back down square, then looked from side to side before leaning into the bars of the window. "Laramie. Both bought tickets to Laramie."

He reached and caught a corner of the bill, but the Professor's finger held it back.

"Did you see them both board the train?"

"Fella, I just sell 'em the tickets. I don't hold their hand to the seat." He pulled the bill free, examined each side of it and yanked it in both directions to make it pop. "Anything else I can help you with?" He tucked the bill inside his jacket. "Hmm?"

"Two tickets to Laramie."

You know, Cooper, I had never ridden on a train before. Wish it hadn't been dark. I would have liked to have seen the scenery. I didn't see squat but the back of the seat in front of me.

At the Laramie station, we stepped onto the platform, and I said, "Now what?"

He spotted the 1st and Kearney sign. "We walk."

# Ten

It didn't take long for Arcadia Vyne to find the Albany County Sheriff's office. "We'll bypass the city police, Baylee," he told me. "Cooper could be anywhere."

We left the dimly lit street and entered into an equally dimly lit lobby. It took about a second to notice the deathly quiet after the creaky door closed. I expected to see someone in uniform behind the counter, but it appeared abandoned. "Maybe they're out looking for bad guys," I said.

"Nonsense." The Professor walked up to the

chest high counter and rapped on the wood. "Service!"

Nothing.

"Does it smell in here to you?" I asked him.

He wrinkled his nose and looked down at our feet. "They's recently put linseed oil on the floor."

"Oh, yeah." I lifted one foot and then the other. "That's what I'm smellin'."

He rapped again. "Service! I want to see the sheriff!"

Something rattled about in a side office.

"Hello!" I cupped my hands over my mouth. "Hello...."

"Keep your shirt on," came a raspy reply. The light extinguished in the office and an ancient man in a gray long sleeve shirt, brown vest, shoestring necktie, and a brown cowboy hat shuffled out. He ignored us and headed to the opposite side of the counter. There must have been some steps back there because when he finally came up even with us, he could look down like a judge ready to pass sentence. "What are you two yelling about out here?" He pulled a red bandanna out of his back pocket and wiped the corners of his mouth.

"I'd like to see your sheriff." The Professor, being taller than me didn't have to crane his neck back as far as I did to see the man behind the counter.

"Are you his deputy?" I asked.

"One of 'em." He pulled a pair of those pinching spectacles off his nose and began to polish them with the bandanna.

"Deputy. My name is Arcadia Vyne. We are from Denver. We have reason to believe a colleague of ours has come to some misfortune in or around this area."

"You don't say?" A stool of some sort scraped the floor behind the counter and the old man worked his way onto it. He still held the high ground. "How long he been missing?"

"Since early this morning."

"Why that ain't no time at all. Why you want and go bother the sheriff about it? You checked all the bars?" He parked the specs back on his nose.

"I'm certain he's not in one of the bars."

The deputy cocked his hat back on his head and revealed some thin strands of hair. "Oh, you are, are you? He some kind of teetotaler?"

"Hey, fella," I said and tried to pull myself a little taller by putting both hands on the edge of the counter. "This gentleman here happens to be the King of Te—"

"Not now, Baylee." The professor pried one of my hands loose and I nearly fell backward.

"Deputy, the sheriff if you please."

"He ain't here."

"I see. When do you expect him to return?"

The old lawman scratched his chin and pondered the ceiling. "Let's see...next week sometime."

"Excuse me?"

"He's gone huntin'. Up in South Dakota. Won't be back till he gets somethin' or somethin' gets him!" A big laugh followed this and then a mumbled, "Somethin' gets him. That's a good one there." Then a cleared throat. "But you might talk to Beuford."

"Beuford?"

"Yeah, Beuford Warner."

"Who is...."

The deputy wiped the corner of his mouth again and leaned forward until it looked like his spectacles would fall off the end of his nose.

"Beuford's the deputy in charge until Sheriff Garland gets back from his huntin' trip. Won't do you no good though. Your friend hasn't been missin' long enough. Right now, he's just not where you can locate him. Wait a while longer and then he'll be missin'."

The Professor took a step back from the counter

and seemed to be setting himself for another try. Sure enough, he took a deep breath, stepped forward and said, "May we then see Deputy Warner."

"He ain't here either."

A crack and then another came from the Professor's thin neck and he angled his head from side to side. "Is he anywhere within walking distance from here?"

"Why sure, he's down at the Buckhorn. 1st and Ivinson. Out the door, turn right. Can't miss it. Follow the piano music."

"Thank you, deputy. You've been most…most helpful."

With that I followed the Professor out the door and we turned right as instructed. Sure enough, we heard a piano not far away and soon we were standing in front of the Buckhorn Bar."

"Let's hope they serve food in here."

"Yeah, I'm starvin', Boss." I opened the door for him and followed into a waft of beer and the aroma and sizzle of steak on an open fire. All but one table was occupied, and a couple of men stood at the bar.

[You were eating steak while I lay tied up with not so much as a stick to gnaw on!]

"I didn't eat until later. You know that!"

[Never mind. Get on with it.]

Anyway, the Professor moved to the bar and asked if Deputy Warner was in the place.

"Beuford?" The bartender chewed on a toothpick and then removed it to point in the direction of the piano. "He's sittin' right there. Red shirt. Tan vest. Under that big Stetson Buffalo."

"A what?" I looked toward the piano. "I don't see nobody wearin' a buffalo."

"The feller in the brown hat, you tinhorn!"

"Oh. Ain't nobody wearin' a brown hat except the guy playin' the piano."

"That's Beuford." The bartender walked away shaking his head. I think he called me something worse than a tinhorn.

The Professor stepped over to the piano and watched the man in the brown hat play. He also wore a rough-looking red shirt with a tan vest, jeans, cowboy boots, and a set of spurs. A droopy hound slept next to his chair, its tail tapping the floor to the music.

When the man finally stopped playing, he turned and spit tobacco juice into a metal can on the floor. "Excuse me there, fella, but you're kinda crowdin' me." That's when I saw his badge. A circle with a star in the middle.

The Professor offered a hand. "Deputy Warner?"

"Friends call me, Beuford. You a friend?" The piano-playing lawman tilted his head, grinned from under his hat, and accepted the Professor's greeting. "What can I do for you?"

"My name is Arcadia Vyne—"

"The Vyne Tea Company?"

The Professor looked startled and took a step back. "Why, yes. Vyne Tea is my family's business. You're familiar with it?"

"Aw, I don't drink it myself. I'm partial to horseshoe coffee. But my wife. She won't drink nothin' else."

"It's a pleasure to meet you, sir." The Professor held out his hand again.

Deputy Beuford wiped his palm on the leg of his jeans and stood as he accepted the shake.

"The deputy down at your office—"

"Ol' Horatio? He's a retired railroad conductor who does a fine job holdin' down that stool behind the counter. He send you over here?"

"Yes. We've come up from Denver looking for a man. A detective in my employee."

The deputy spit in his can again and sleeved his chin. "Thought those detectives were supposed to look for people, not be the ones looked for."

"Yes, I suppose that is the usual case. We think

Cooper may have been following someone and ran into trouble perhaps. There's even a chance he was on the trail of another missing person, a Miss Rowena Preston."

"Was he out to search Laramie specifically, or Wyoming in general?"

"He bought a ticket to Laramie. After that? Our trail turned cold, I'm afraid."

The bartender, who had worked his way back down the bar and apparently overheard the conversation, threw a thumb over his shoulder. "Maybe he's that 'wolf man' those boys saw."

This brought a round of guffaws and snorts from the other diners and drinkers in the room.

"Those young'uns sure spun a tale this morning," one of the men said around a mouthful of beef.

"They had an imagination, I'll give 'em that," added another.

I was eyeing that ribeye on the guy's plate when the Professor stepped forward. "Boys? Wolf man?"

Deputy Beuford waved them off. "Them kids was just yappin' a story so Doc Dorsey would buy em' a sody water."

"Yeah, to hear Doc repeat what they told him, I thought my side was gonna' split wide open." This from the bartender. "I saw that *Werewolf of London* over at the Princess Theater in Cheyenne a couple or three years ago. Scared the tar out of my old lady. What those three squirts were describin' didn't look nothin' like the fiend in that movie."

"Professor, I saw that movie too." I shivered. "This guy goes to Tibet, lookin' for this flower and when he gets back—"

"Yes, Baylee, you can tell me all about it later." He returned his attention to Deputy Beuford. "Just what did these lads say?"

The lawman sat on his chair and bent to rub the hound's ears with both hands. "There were three of them. Not older than ten or eleven. They hang out around Doc Dorsey's place 'cause he'll give 'em a treat for a good story. Well, the Doc tells us these kids had been up at the ag station, the place what used to be a prison—"

"The Territorial Prison?"

"Yeah, that's the place. The towheaded one was doin' all the talkin'." He looked at the bartender. "What did Doc say that kid's name is?"

"Freddy Hobson, I think he said."

"Yeah, Freddy. Ancel Hobson's kid. Must get his gift of gab from Ancel, that man can talk circles around you if you let him. Anyway, Freddy tells

Doc that he and his buddies were up at the station messin' around and they found this man in a cage. Said he was all wild. Clothes tore off of him. Crazy lookin'. He tried to get them to come over to the cage so he could eat them. Said he was talkin' some kind of foreign language." Beuford Warner laughed. "I told you they were spinnin' a tale. Then they started talkin' about the wolf. It just appeared. Doc asked them how it got out of the cage, but they were a little vague on that part."

"When did all this happen?" The Professor leaned in for a response.

"Doc said this morning."

"Where is this Freddy. This Freddy...."

"Hobson."

"Freddy Hobson." The Professor turned to me. "Baylee we may be back on the trail."

"Well, by now he's probably in bed, dreamin' about that wolf man."

"Deputy, I think those boys may have seen our man, Jonas Cooper. Can you take me to this boy's house?"

The lawman scratched the hound's ears a final time. "I'll do you one better, Mr. Vyne. We'll load up and go over to the station. We'll just see if we can find us a wolf man ourselves."

We made our way out of the bar and Deputy Beuford led us to a Marmon-Herrington converted Ford half-ton truck. He turned and yelled back through the door, "Somebody go down and tell ol' Horatio I'm takin' these two fellers out to the Big Stink."

Under the streetlight, the vehicle looked rough for its age. Open in the front, with a canopy over the back, I knew we were in for a ride.

He pointed the Professor into the front passenger seat and me into the back. A little higher body than your average car, I had to heft myself up and over the side onto a canvas tarpaulin which appeared to cover three or four crates as I could see the corners of some of them. This made for a dandy seat until the old hound came out and Deputy Beuford picked the dog up and shoved him up over the side, almost into my lap.

The motor fired and black smoke came up through the floorboard. "Hang on!" he yelled and jabbed the stick shift into first gear and ground the clutch in the process. With headlights now on, we headed for the agricultural station.

"Sunday night, shouldn't be anybody up there." His jerky clutch forced a shift into second. "Just students up there on the weekend. They check the stock off and on. Different ones each week." A hard push into third and we picked up speed. "But you know them kids. Don't pay no more attention to what's goin' on around them than a hog at a feed trough. They got just one thing on their mind at a time. That and they want to get their chores done as fast as possible cause they got a hot date."

We were soon pulling up to a big sandstone building. A couple or more stories high. Next to this were all these pens with cattle and beyond that, another building.

Deputy Beuford drove around the pens and pulled up to one of the small buildings. There were a couple of barn doors side by side and some windows. It was creepy dark. He downshifted to slow us and then stomped on the brake pedal. A moment later he killed the engine, and the creepy dark was joined by a creepy almost silence full of bug noises and snoring cows. How that old hound slept through the entire trip, I'll never know.

A bit of wind whipped up and some of these round weed-looking things bounced and rolled into the vehicle.

"Welcome to the Wyoming Territorial Prison, gentlemen. Currently known as the University of

Wyoming Agricultural Experiment Station. I call it the Big Stink." He crawled out of the driver's seat and his spurs jingled as he spit. "Butch Cassidy himself was incarcerated here a little over forty years ago. It was a state prison then. My old man was a guard here before they closed it down and eventually moved all this livestock in."

"What's that horrible smell?" I held a hand over my nose.

"Told ya, cows and such."

With the headlights still on we could see through the dirty windows of the building.

The Professor worked his way out of the vehicle and Deputy Beuford pointed at the passenger seat. "Rumage under there, you might find a flashlight. But mind the bear trap." He then slapped the side of his leg, and the old hound worked its way from the back to the front where it received some assistance to the ground. "That's a good ol' son." The deputy scruffed its ears.

The Professor did as instructed and worked his long gangly arm underneath and extracted a flashlight that looked like it came with the vehicle. It put out a pretty good beam and soon we had the barn doors open and went inside.

"Why are we going in here?" I asked and looked

about into the shadows. "Why not over into the big building?"

Deputy Beuford shrugged and led the way. "Good place to start as any, I guess."

The Professor's flashlight cast a beam across the floor. "Is that a printing press?"

"They use it to print pamphlets and things for the station. How to plant beans, stuff like that." He worked his way around the walls until he came back to the same place. "There's been a lot of something moved out of here recently. Look at all the drag marks in the dust on the floor. And tire tracks. They backed in here and loaded whatever it was. In a hurry too, by the looks of how everything else is knocked over."

"Well, Jonas isn't in here," said the Professor as he inspected the press. "Let's move on."

The headlights coming through the window started to dim.

"I better go out and shut those off." Deputy Beuford headed for the door with the hound at his heels. "Else, it'll run the battery down. You two go on over and I'll be along after you." He spit into one of the tire tracks. "Sure can't figure out what they moved out of here so fast. Not likely anything for the station. Your fella may have well been here and came across something he wasn't supposed to."

"All right. Baylee, let's go see what's over in the bigger building." The Professor led the way with the flashlight. "If Jonas did stumble upon something here, I doubt they took him with them."

"You think they made him load all of whatever it was they loaded?"

"Perhaps."

"Maybe they took him to unload it somewhere else."

"They were printing something they didn't want anyone to find. My guess, something counterfeit. Money perhaps. But whatever, they wouldn't want a witness to tell the tale."

I gulped. "Professor, you're not sayin'...."

"We should prepare for the worst."

"Oh, man." I stood stock still for a moment, but he was off, and I followed him. I didn't want to follow him. I didn't want to....

"Baylee, keep up!"

"Yes, sir." That's when I spotted your hat under the printing press. "Hey! Look!"

He played the beam of light under the press.

"He's been here. We can now be sure of it."

I retrieved your hat and followed him. In the bigger building he directed the flashlight up into the corners of the first area we came into.

Some kind of cage hung on the walls above us.

I came in close behind him and whispered, "What kind of place is this, Professor?"

"The deputy said it was an old prison. Those would be where the guards would watch down on the convicts."

"They locked the guards up too?"

He turned and pointed the light into my face. "Don't be ridiculous, young man."

I stepped to one side, "But the cage—"

"Has doors to come and go through the back. See?" The light moved in a circle and illuminated the interior of the metal enclosure.

"Oh, yeah. Right." I kicked some straw. "Maybe we should go up there for a better look."

"We'll proceed down here for the moment." With that he moved ahead and worked his light along the straw covered floor. "Baylee, see those drag marks? They've pulled something heavy through here."

We followed those until we came across the first of a line of cells in the wall. The first one empty. The second one empty. The third one....

"Cooper! Professor, it's Cooper. We've found him!"

# ELEVEN

They'd found me all right. Unconscious.

When I'd made my way through the haze, and back to the realm of the living, I realized they'd pulled me out of the cell. Something wet licked its way across my forehead. I squinted up at four faces in a little circle of light coming from the Professor's hand, his gaunt grin a sight to see as he worked himself between me and the face with dropping ears and a cold nose.

Baylee, eyes searching, knelt beside me. "Cooper, what did they do to you?" He pulled the gag from my mouth. "You look like something chewed on you and spit you out. Was it the wolf man?"

"Don't let this one feed you that kid's story," said a man in a red shirt and tan vest who held out his hand to help me to my feet. I also noticed the jingle of spurs. The sleepy dog and head of the welcoming committee stood at his side and drooled. "Mr. Cooper, you gave these two fellers' a fright tonight."

The Professor turned the light to the cowboy's weathered face. "Jonas, this is Deputy Beuford Warner. He aided us in finding you."

"Pleased to meet you, Deputy. Can't say I think much of your prison facilities here. The floor is really uncomfortable, and the meals are nonexistent." His handshake was firm. "And to top it off, you got crime going on right next door." I steadied myself and attempted to take a step. "Come on, I'll show you."

"No need, son." The deputy retrieved my suit coat, then threw a thumb over his shoulder. "Whatever it was, they've cleared out."

"Jonas." The Professor held me by my forearm. "We need to know something. Do you know anything about Rowena?"

I ran my free hand over my head from front to

neck and came back with straw. Rowena? Who's Rowena?"

"You know her, Cooper." Baylee started slapping dust off of my clothes and parked my hat on my head.

"I do?"

"Mr. and Mrs. Preston's daughter. From next door."

"The old maid?"

"She's not so old."

"She will be before she ever lands a husband."

"Rowena is missing, Jonas. We thought you might have been trying to find her."

I shook my head as I pushed Baylee away and took over the dusting. "No, I was tailing Brock Sanderson's loud tie."

"Loud tie, you say?" This from the deputy.

"Did I say loud? More like a screamer. Ugliest tie this side of the Rockies."

"'Bout five-eight?" The deputy rubbed his chin. "Full of himself and thinks he looks tough?"

"Have you seen this man, deputy?" asked the Professor.

"He was struttin' into the barbershop this evening. Was walkin' in as I was walkin' out."

This perked my interest and gave me a bit of an

adrenalin rush. Enough to help steady my feet. Enough to let me know my stomach felt nauseous from lack of food. "Where did he go after that?"

"No idea. Didn't give him a second thought."

"You could of arrested him for wearing that tie."

Deputy Warner laughed. "Ain't no law against bad taste in this county."

"Remind me to talk to your elected officials." I kicked at the straw on the floor. Let's get out of here. I need food. I've been smellin' cows for the last day. Anybody know where I can get a steak?"

The trio exchanged glances.

"I know just the place," volunteered the deputy.

"Oh, man!" Baylee licked his lips and rubbed his hands together.

"You know something I don't?" I grabbed the little guy by the shoulder for support.

"This thick, Cooper." He held up his thumb and forefinger with a questionable gap between them. "Pan-fried potatoes too."

"Beans," chimed in the lawman. "Don't forget the beans, young man."

"Oh, yeah. Beans, Cooper. Plates and plates of beans."

I grabbed Baylee's other shoulder and turned

him on his heels. "Quit torturing me! I've had enough of that already. Lead on to this cookery. This Wyoming oasis."

The hound came to life and bayed like he'd caught a scent. He wobbled to his four feet and trotted ahead of us and out beyond the edge of the flashlight's reach.

❦

As advertised, the Buckhorn proved to be the best meal I'd had since last week. As a matter of fact, it was the only meal I'd had since last week. Three thick T-bone steaks took up all the real estate on three plates before us. Myself, Baylee, and Deputy Beuford sawed and chewed as I related everything from the lineup to the three boys and the wolf.

There's one thing you can say about Mr. Arcadia Vyne and that is he never lets the help go hungry, although for himself he had a small sirloin that looked like a trial version of the behemoths before the rest of us.

At an adjacent table he trimmed, cut, and chewed methodically and wished out loud more than once to the bartender that the Buckhorn could produce a single cup of hot tea.

Finally, with about half his meal untouched, he

lowered the big sharp steak knife to the side of his plate and looked over at me. "Jonas, what were they printing on that press?"

Around a mouthful of hot apple pie, I answered. "Stock certificates." Another bite. Then a swig of the most awful coffee I had ever encountered. Hot. Good. "And by the reaction of Sanderson when he compared it to a real one, they were more than passable. Crates of em'."

"Stock certificates?" asked Baylee, his own mouth full of pie. "What can they do with phony certificates?"

"Plenty," offered the deputy. "Get em' out into circulation and water down the price of the real ones. If they can sell them quick, they'll make a hundred percent profit and cheat a lot of honest folks out of their old age mattress money."

"Jonas, did you see a company on the certificates?"

"Just a glance. I was about to get a good look and Sanderson got another idea." I stretched my arms over my head until my spine popped. "I think it was Mustang something."

"Mustang Gap Mining?"

"Could have been."

"Oh, dear."

"Bad news, Mr. Vyne?" The deputy pushed his chair away from the table, sliced a plug of tobacco with his steak knife, and parked the chaw in his cheek.

"Yes, if those certificates are for Mustang Gap Mining, we can expect more terrible things to happen. Jonas, I think you've discovered the reason for Rowena Preston's sudden disappearance. Plus, the reason they left you alive in that cell."

I let the bite of pie fall from my fork. "Spill, Professor. What's the angle?"

"You remember that obituary you read Saturday morning?"

Baylee shook his head. "Please don't get him started with that again."

"Seriously, Jonas. The notice of the death of my old friend Norbert Olympus Bodie?"

"Yeah." I nodded to agree. "No body."

"Nobody?" The deputy's eyebrows arched. "You kiddin'?'"

"On the contrary, deputy. N. O. Bodie was a major stockholder in the Mustang Gap Mining Company. In fact, he held the second largest block."

"Who owns the most?" I asked.

"I do."

"You?"

"Yes, I am the major holder."

"You own more than half of it all?" asked Baylee.

"No, my boy that would be a majority holder. I do, however, own the largest block of stocks. There are a few other major holders. Jonas, I think that's why you were led up here. To get you out of the way."

I pushed my chair away from the table. "Hey, wait a cotton pickin' second there. Nobody led me…. I mean I wasn't led up here. It was a legitimate tail. Sanderson had no idea I was…. Well, I don't think he did." I settled back into my chair. "Now that you mention it…."

"With you missing, they could use that against me."

The clouds were parting. "Let me guess, the next biggest holder is —"

"Yes. It's Evangeline Preston. Rowena Preston's mother."

"Evangeline?" I asked. "What about Preston himself?"

The Professor shook his head. "She inherited her money. He married it."

"Hmm…. Interesting. How many other big stockholders are we talkin' about here, Professor?"

"At the most, four. Gerald Myton, Elias Erdody,

Holbrook Thompson Bahr, and his sister Thessaly Neufeld."

"And I'm guessin' they all have a close relative that might just somehow manage to walk off the face of the earth."

The Professor's brows furrowed. "Yes."

"But why?"

"The annual stockholders meeting is this Tuesday. Scheduled far in advance of N. O.'s passing. Someone wants to sabotage that meeting."

"But isn't Bodie's stock suddenly all tied up. Probate? Wills? Court stuff?"

"If the person we are up against is smart, they can use that to their advantage."

"And flood the market and make the stock worthless?" asked the deputy.

"Yes."

"Well, don't that beat all?" He turned his chin over his shoulder and managed to spit in the can from where he sat.

Vyne nodded. "You're very astute deputy. I'm impressed.

The burly man pushed his Stetson back on his head. "Some cowpokes manage to squeeze in a degree in Economics when there's a good school in town."

"Remind me to never underestimate you, sir."

"And who inherits Bodie's stock?" I asked to get us all back on track. "Professor?"

"I'm not sure, but I have an idea. If it's who I think it is and she's behind this.... We have a lot to do in a short amount of time. N. O.'s funeral is also scheduled for Tuesday in the lobby of the Mining Exchange after the close of trading. The stockholders' meeting is later that evening in the boardroom of the same building. Between now and then we not only need to locate Rowena, but we'll also need to find the four other kidnapped victims."

"What four others?" Baylee had been holding his coffee cup in front of his face for a while, mesmerized by the unfolding scenario. "I've been with you the whole time and you've never mentioned four others. How do you know? When were they kidnapped?"

Vyne pulled his watch from his pocket and consulted the time. "I would hazard to guess, right about now." He looked around. I need a phone. "I think I will send Stewart to the Sanatorium to alert them to keep an eye on my sister, Ardith."

# Twelve

The police take a dim view of you reporting a crime before it happens. Detective Burgess Raft was no exception.

Deputy Beuford Warner had been kind enough to transport us all back to Denver and plant us on Raft's jailhouse doorstep. We'd spent the night in a downtown Laramie hotel and had departed after breakfast. When Vyne had called Stewart to tell him I'd been found and to check on his sister, the Professor inquired as to the status of Rowena Preston. No change.

As we watched the deputy drive away, it seemed

like I'd just left this spot on the tail of Sanderson.

Raft didn't appear all that glad to see me again. "So, they found you, did they?" He lit his pipe and motioned for us to sit. "Wandered off into the foothills, did you?"

"More like kidnapped and trussed up like a rodeo calf in a ropin' contest." I tilted my chair back and put my big shoes up on his big desk.

He flicked his match at me and caused me to remove them. "I'd like to have seen that."

I worked my head from side to side and rubbed my neck. "The key word in my statement is 'Kidnap'." I spelled it out slowly. "K-I-D-N-A-P."

"All this took place in Laramie, you say?"

"They locked him up in that old prison," volunteered Baylee. "The one full of cows."

Raft cracked a sly smile. "Now there's a new one. Prison full of cows. I bet you fit right in, Cooper." He waved a hand of dismissal at me. "Not in my jurisdiction. Not a thing I can do about it. Try to get yourself kidnapped in the city limits next time."

"Well, what about Rowena?" This again from Baylee.

For some reason Vyne sat very still and didn't seem to be engaged in the conversation. He kinda stared at the wall over Raft's head.

"And who, young man, is this Rowena? And what about her am I supposed to know?"

"Rowena Preston." Baylee stood, put his palms on Raft's desk, and leaned toward him. "She's missing. Didn't her parents call you?"

Raft stared him back into his chair. "First I've heard of it." He flagged an officer near his door. "Morris!"

"Yes, sir?"

"Foot it down to the desk, ask the sergeant if we've had any calls from some folks named Preston."

"Yes, sir."

"Kidnapped too?"

I wasn't sure who he directed the question to, so I spoke up with what information Vyne and Baylee had filled me in on. "There's a good possibility."

"Is this Rowena a child?"

"She's an adult," I said.

"She has all her wits about her?"

I shrugged. "As far as I know."

"Then why," he huffed, "does she need her parents to keep up with her?"

"Well, I don't suppose she does —"

He waved me off. "And you think there's going to be more? More kidnappings?" He said this in reference to the story we told him to get us into his office.

"Possibly four or five."

"And you say you know who is going to be kidnapped?"

"We think so."

Arcadia Vyne cleared his throat. Back with the living he held up his hand and counted off on his left hand with the tip of his right index finger. "Gerald Myton, who owns the Myton auto dealership, has a son named Arthur. Age mid-twenties. Up and comer Elias Erdody, who has a fleet of airplanes flying all over Colorado, has a young sister. I believe her name is Ava. She's around nineteen or so. Then there's Holbrook Bahr and his daughter, Janet. Thirty-five. Bahr's sister, Thessaly Neufeld, just married a man half her age, named Thorndike. He's twenty-nine and looks nineteen. The Bahr siblings own several hotels and restaurants. They all have money, and they all have something in common with myself and the Prestons."

"Which is?" Smoke wisped over the Detective's head and set out for an open window.

"We all own large blocks of stock in the Mustang Gap Mining Company, and we are all scheduled to attend a shareholders meeting tomorrow evening.

Oh, and we might also add Millicent Mundene, née Bodie, to the list."

"And who's she?"

"Shouldn't you be writing this down?" I asked.

"And who's she?" Raft asked again.

"The grandniece and sole heir of N. O. Bodie."

"The big shot who died the other day?"

Morris, who'd been sent to the sergeant's desk for information, had just entered the office.

Raft looked past me to the cop at the door. "What did you find out, Morris?"

"Patrolman Feilding was sent to the Preston's home, sir. He reported they didn't make a lot of sense."

"Report a kidnapping?"

"They talked about a daughter. Walks and library books. He advised to give it some time."

The detective waved a dismissive hand at the officer. "There you are, Vyne. No kidnappings reported in my city. You're wasting my time."

The Professor huffed and looked perturbed. The Prestons are…. There was a note. Why didn't they…?" He tapped on the desktop with his boney index finger. "I'd like you to at least send some men around to check on these people I've mentioned."

"You've mentioned more people than I have the

manpower to cover on my meager budget. And why these specific relatives? What makes them so special?" At last, Raft seemed to show some half-hearted interest.

Vyne held out his hands wide in front of him. "Simple. Obvious."

"Not to me." Raft growled the words and the moment of interest appeared to wane.

"Each one is about the same age range as Cooper here, and Rowena Preston. Each would be missed in a short amount of time. Each would be dear enough to warrant the possibility of blackmail."

I turned my head to stare directly at Vyne. "I didn't know you cared."

"If it hadn't been you, it would have been Stewart, or Baylee, or Rodrick. I don't have any close family here, except for my sister, Ardith, in the Sanatorium. She's too weak for them to take."

Baylee didn't like what he heard. "You mean it could have been me all tied up in that stinkin' —"

"Enough!" Raft leaned forward. The bowl of his pipe glowed bright red. "Who do you suppose is doing all this alleged carrying off of people and planned carrying off of people?"

"I have my suspicions," said Vyne.

"Care to share?"

"Not at this moment."

The police detective shook his head. "You three take the cake. You want me to expend valuable manpower to investigate an unreported kidnapping, head half a dozen more off at the pass, and find the guy behind it all. Three crazy loons, I'm looking at. And I'm getting mighty tired of it."

The Professor's expression never changed.

"There's Sanderson." I pointed in the general direction of where I thought the lineup room might be.

"You said he left the state."

"He may have returned."

"May have?"

"There's the sourdough stock certificates."

"It just gets better and better, doesn't it?"

"We all saw the printing press." We all nodded in agreement.

Raft pulled the pipe from his lips and slammed it down on the desk. "For all you know he might have been printing play money for Christmas morning!" He eyed what was left of the pipe. Broken stem over by Baylee, bowl and scattered smoldering tobacco next to his candlestick phone. He stood and pointed at the door. "Get out! Somebody open some more windows! Smells like a feedlot in here! Take a bath, the bunch of you!"

We hurried through the door before he hurled something else as he yelled, "My mother gave me that pipe!"

⁂

Once again out on the steps of the Denver Police Station, Baylee said, "What do we do now?"

I stayed back in the shadows of the doorway. "Professor?"

"Yes, Jonas?"

"It seems to me," I said pointing out into the world, "that Sanderson and his thugs don't know I've broke jail. As far as they know, I'm still up there in Laramie. Doubt if they ever give it a second thought to send someone up there to check on my well-being. I have a pretty good impression Sanderson passed a death sentence on me."

"You may be right." Vyne looked up and down the street. "Baylee, get the car please. Jonas, stay against the door until he pulls up."

Baylee hotfooted it down to the corner and soon Vyne's green '32 900 Light Eight Roadster rolled in front of the curb near the steps. He stepped around from the driver's seat and held the rear door open for Vyne. When all appeared clear on the coast, they both waved for me to make it to the backseat.

Once inside I slid down so my head couldn't be seen through the windows or back glass.

Baylee returned to the driver's seat and restarted the engine. I really wanted to take a detour to the hospital to see Mary but decided not to chance it. For the foreseeable future I needed to make like Claude Rains in *The Invisible Man*.

❦⁂❧

When we arrived at the back of the House of Vyne we unloaded and made our way in through the kitchen door.

Stewart looked up from helping Dotty the cook put away some fresh vegetables.

Rick sat at the table. "Back already?"

"I missed you too, old chap." I looked in the grocery box and found an apple.

"Honestly, Cooper. I was concerned. It's hard for Dotty to plan a meal when she doesn't know how many to serve."

I went over and gave the old woman a big kiss on the cheek. "Plan extra helpings for me, sweetheart. All I've had to eat for the last day or so is half a cow and a bucket of beans. I'm still hungry."

She laughed and blushed and with a good knowledge of her employer's needs, filled a kettle with water for tea and put it on the stove to heat.

"So, what's our next move, Professor?" I asked.

He motioned for Baylee and pointed out the window toward the garage. "After we have a cup of tea, we're going to have to do what the police are not willing to."

"And that is?" I asked as I watched Baylee nod and head for the door.

"We need to first find out why the Prestons didn't tell the police about the ransom note." He looked at Stewart. "I'm correct in assuming there's no change. She's not back?"

"Yes, sir."

He looked at me. "And what about the others on our list? Are they safe?"

"We could call."

"I think it best if we observe their homes and watch for any strange activity. I don't want to alert them if there's no need."

"But you're pretty sure there's going to be a need."

"Yes."

"That's going to take some time to get around to all of them. We can't watch everyone at once."

"Agreed." He clasped his hands. "Can you as-semble a group of operatives to help us with this surveillance?."

"Sure," I nodded. "We've got a club. I'll go down and give the secret handshake."

He gave me his 'this is serious' stare.

"I'll see what I can do. But it will have to be on the Q. T. what with me having to be unseen and all."

"Good, we've got till tomorrow to find out if any more people have been taken. Then we have to find Rowena, and the others perhaps, which I would surmise may all be at the same location."

"Not to mention why all this is happening. And who is behind it?"

"Exactly."

"I'll start making some phone calls. What are you going to do?"

"I need to think for a while."

He was good at thinkin' and I was better at action. "Okay, we've got a plan," I told him. "Now it's off to my abode above the carriage house for a bath and a shave."

# THIRTEEN

**A** good hot bath will usually ease the crick in your back, but I had the crick of all cricks and pulling on clean duds proved more painful than when I peeled off the dirty ones.

There's something about being all tied up that misaligns your joints and your bones. I feared it might be a couple of days before I popped everything back into their original positions.

After I halfway whipped up a cup of shaving cream and scrapped the thickening shadow off the lower part of my face with the results, I held a towel under the hot water in the sink and then draped it over my head. This helped a bit with the lingering headache. I tilted my head to and fro and got a good crack in return. This helped too.

Feeling somewhat more presentable I made my way back to the main house and found Vyne, Stewart, Rodrick, and Baylee feasting on sandwiches and hot tea in the dining room. Dotty, bless her heart, had set a carafe of coffee next to my plate of assorted meats, cheeses, and slices of bread. After an initial swig of coffee, I proceeded to arrange everything into a sandwich Dagwood Bumstead would be proud of.

While we ate, Caffeine the cat appeared and did figure eights around all our legs under the table. A few bossy "meows" garnered a bit of cheese and a sliver of ham.

Meal complete and aftermath cleared, we sat with ears wide open as Arcadia Vyne plotted our battle plan for the afternoon.

First order of business was a discussion of Rodrick's update on the Prestons, which he had presented during the meal. "They remain highly distraught." He repeated from earlier.

"Did they still have the note?" Vyne asked.

"Mrs. Preston had it in her hand. She waved it about, but I didn't see it open."

"They didn't mention any ransom demand?"

"No, sir. They seemed perplexed. They were told Rowena had been taken. They were told she was safe but under guard somewhere. They were told they must attend Mr. Bodie's funeral tomorrow evening and the stockholder's meeting after that. If they failed to do those two things, they would never see her again."

"These crooks know that under the circumstance and the stress the last thing the Prestons would do would be to go out," Vyne said. "Practicality would encourage them to stay home and wait for another contact. Did they say why they didn't show the note to the police?"

"Yes, sir." Rodrick leaned forward. "She indicated the note specifically told them the police were not to be notified. But you insisted. So, they did, sans showing them the note. "

"I see."

I rapped on the table. "We have to assume they're watching the Preston's house."

"Agreed." Vyne nodded. "They will be watching the other houses as well. We took a chance sending over Rodrick. We'll have to be more cautious when we contact the others."

"Goons out on the street can't hear phone calls."

"Yes, but what if they've tapped their lines or have someone listening in at windows?"

Baylee chimed in. "We all wear fake mustaches!"

"I just shaved," I shot back. "Not going to wear a fake mustache."

"The young man is on to something there." This from Vyne.

"Really?" This from myself and Baylee at the same time.

Vyne stood and walked slowly around and around the table on his gangly stork-like legs. It didn't help the crick in my neck any as I tried to keep my eyes on him.

"If they've taken a family member and if they're watching the house," he said to no one in particular during this dining room circular stroll, "and if they've delivered a similar note, they'll be wise to anyone trying to make contact and we won't be able to approach the houses because they know who we are."

"Take a breath, Professor," I said. "That all makes sense. But we've got to get in there somehow and get some info."

"And here's how we do it." Vyne smiled. "Thanks to Baylee."

# FOURTEEN

I didn't have a bit of luck hiring extra men, especially trying to keep it covert. So, we were on our own.

Our first house, a trial run, was located on Grant Street.

Rick appeared around the corner astride a brand-new Shelby Supreme Airflow Bicycle.

Vyne had bought the red beauty right out of the shop window. A phoneyed up white uniform came next and then a bright bouquet of flowers to finish the disguise.

We sat in Vyne's '32 900 Light Eight Roadster far

enough away that we needed binoculars and watched Rodrick's performance. Sitting stock straight on the spring leather saddle seat, one hand on the right handlebar's black grip, the other holding the paper-wrapped flowers at attention, Rick coasted to a stop where the path to the front door met the sidewalk adjacent to a wrought iron fence with small rose bushes planted every foot or so. He awkwardly toed the stand up under the back wheel and although we couldn't hear him, he looked to be whistling as he approached the front door under an awning that looked like half a turtle shell guarded by two white globe lanterns.

Across and down a bit a '34 Cadilac sedan sat with another interested party. He also possessed binoculars.

"I think the bad guys have this one in their bag," I told Vyne and Baylee from the back seat where I hunched down and parked my own binoculars on the cushions of the front. "Let's hope they buy Mr. Rick's little melodrama."

Gerald Myton's manservant answered the door. I hoped he didn't give it away right off. You gotta figure that one rich man's help can spot another's at fifty paces. But maybe they had a secret wink or something because Rick boldly presented the flowers with a pre-scripted insistence that Gerald Myton and no other could take possession. 'The sender insisted' he'd been instructed to say.

Myton's man shook his head and held out his hand to accept the delivery.

Rick stood his ground, puffed out his chest, and waved an arm about. He also pointed a lot. None of these things seemed to have any effect.

Eventually Myton's man took a straight step back into the house and shut the door.

Our phony delivery guy stood tall as a Buckingham guard and didn't glance around.

"Good goin', Mr. Rick," I said. "Not givin' yourself or us away."

A full two minutes passed, and the door opened again.

"That's Gerald Myton," confirmed Vyne, of the man whose tan was whiter than Rick's uniform.

More pointing on the porch, but we knew this time it wasn't about who would take possession of the flowers. Rick was asking him about relatives, kidnappings, and notes.

Myton bought into the charade and started to communicate with his hands and arms as well. He seemed to be trying to tell Rick that the delivery went to the next house down. We hoped he was filling our man in on the particulars. Rick would in turn tell him that Arcadia Vyne and crew were in the process of sorting it all out.

Finally, Myton waved Rick off in mock disgust, turned, reentered the big house, and slammed the door so hard our man had to take a step back. It appeared the message had been delivered.

Rick looked at the flowers, then at the door, and then over the bushes to the house along the way. He retreated down the path, bypassed his bicycle, and found the corresponding path to the next house. After several minutes of banging the knocker against the door and toe tapping, he shrugged, returned to his bicycle with flowers in hand, disengaged the kick stand from under the back wheel, mounted, and returned the way he came.

"Oh, great!" I let the binoculars slip from my fingers into the front seat.

Baylee grabbed them up. "What?"

"The bicycle. Price tag's still dangling by a string from the handlebars."

❦

Baylee pulled up to the curb a few blocks away. Mr. Rick stood waiting for us. I reached to push the rear passenger side door open, and he ducked in and closed it behind him.

Before we even asked, he started his report. "They've got Myton's son Arthur for sure. He didn't return from the cinema last evening. They received a similar note with the same instructions as the Prestons."

"Have they called the police?" Vyne had turned himself so he could see us in the back seat.

"No, sir. Too afraid."

"Do they have any idea where they might have taken young Arthur?"

"No, sir."

"We need to find out about the others as soon as we can. Baylee are you ready to do what we discussed?"

"Time to visit Elias Erdody?"

"Exactly."

I held up a hand. "Now hold on a second, let's work this out. We could cover more ground if we didn't visit them in turn. Each of us take one."

"They all know me," countered Vyne.

"And I'm known by the Erdodys," added Rick.

"If these reprobates are coordinating with each other and they catch on…. The game's a bust. Visiting them one at a time gives them more time to, well what I'm saying is, it just takes one genius in the bunch to put two and two together. We strike fast, get our information, then back away – less time."

"Or," said Vyne, "they are coordinating and all of the sudden everyone they're watching gets a visit at the same time. Similar results."

"So, it's six of one and half a dozen of the other."

"Essentially."

"Then what are we going to do?"

"First, Rodrick is going to load his bicycle and then we head to the Erdody Estate."

❧❦❧

We arrived at said 'Estate' and palatial didn't begin to describe this spread on Wadsworth Boulevard.

You couldn't see the house from the road because of the fruit trees and marble statuary. We figured between ourselves that they probably had one of their spies hole up on the grounds somewhere.

Baylee drove on by, went about a mile, and then after a sloppy three-point turnabout, rolled a bit down the hill with the motor off.

No bicycle for this job. Baylee's assignment was easy. Walk the rest of the way along the road, admire the sprawling gate a bit too much, trip on a nonexistent crack, and sprain his ankle within crawling range of the intercom box.

Spencer Tracy couldn't have pulled off a better performance.

The intercom button pushed, a plea for help, and soon a gardener appeared and opened the gate. The gardener, not being a doctor, examined Baylee's supposed injury and eventually motioned for him to stay propped up against the ornamental gate post.

Soon Elias Erdody appeared in his chauffeured Rolls Royce. Again, Baylee and the man must have had the secret club sign because they seemed none the wiser. As Erdody examined the ankle, he was fed the prearranged questions.

After a few minutes Erdody had the gardener, who'd reappeared, and his chauffeur load Baylee up into the big car. The engine roared to life and departed, leaving Erdody behind. He shook his head and motioned for the gardener to close the gate and then he walked back toward his home.

Baylee had done such a convincing job that with Rodrick driving we had to follow the Rolls all the way to the hospital.

His report echoed the previous one at Myton's except this time it was, as Vyne predicted, Erdody's younger sister Ava, age thirty, who'd been snatched from near the porch of her piano teacher's home as she walked to her little sporty convertible. Same instructions. Attend Mr. Bodie's funeral and the stockholder's meeting after that. Even though the notes said nothing about refraining from calling the police, each had read it as an implied meaning.

❦

The story held true at the home of Holbrook Bahr in the northwest part of the city where indeed his twenty-one-year-old daughter, Janet, had not returned from her volunteer job at the nearby elementary school.

Vyne batted a thousand when we next discovered that Thorndike Neufeld had disappeared from the loving arms of his older bride, Thessaly Bahr Neufeld. Apparently at gunpoint.

This left one last stop. The heir of N. O. Bodie. Vyne was most wary of this one as it would be the most difficult to verify. There was no one to try to get close to and ask. She lived in the Brown Palace Hotel and to ascertain if she'd been kidnapped along with the others would entail getting up to her room, breaking in, and searching for some evidence. A thousand things could go wrong. Baylee and Rick had both taken turns at playacting and now it rested on me to do my part.

This woman wouldn't know me from Adam. We agreed, however, that going up as myself or going up as someone who would blend in gave us different options. We finally settled on my posing as a waiter from the kitchen if – and it was a big if – I could sneak a uniform out of the kitchen that fit.

⁂

We decided I'd go in late when the kitchen had all but closed after the dining room dinner time. This left no more than a few staff doing cleanup and taking items up for room service.

I figured this gag would be as easy as falling off a log, if the log were made outta metal and I had magnets in my shoes.

One of the waiters I had observed stood about my height and size so when he came out of a small employee breakroom in street clothes I knew I could get his uniform of the day out of the bin instead of trying to figure out which locker was his. Not that I relished the notion of wearing another guy's sweaty togs, but he'd appeared to have managed not to get soup on him and they were still presentable. Burgandy pants, matching vest, and a white long-sleeved shirt. It just took a bit of smoothing out on a table to get them back in shape. The fit felt a bit snug, and I noticed my shoes didn't have enough shine to pull off the charade.

A fancy linen napkin and a bit of spit proved to be the ticket for a quick buff.

The most difficult touch turned out to be the bow tie as it took several attempts to get it right without a mirror and two attempts after I found my reflection in a shiny metal pot.

A little desk occupied the corner, apparently where the chef planned his menus. A pair of round reading glasses sat atop a stack of produce receipts. Perched on my nose, I could just see over the tops without having to look through them. The chef these belonged to had quite an eyesight problem and with them up in front of my eyes the world blurred and became unnavigable.

Next, I needed a tray and a cart. I didn't want to have to balance the thing with one hand and putting it on a cart allowed me to bend a bit at the waist so as not to have to make direct eye contact with anyone as I would have to do if I stood spine straight.

In the next room over I found what I needed. The staff had now moved out of the kitchen and into the dining room to prepare it for the next morning. With the tray and the cart in place, complete with a fresh white cover, I set out to find something to put on it.

Not sure how far this ruse would need to go I didn't want to take the chance of not having something that looked like a legitimate room service delivery.

In a big refrigerator I found a cheese tray, a jar of olives, and another jar of some of those funny little pickles. I dumped a handful of each into some glass fruit cups and stuck toothpicks in a couple of them. Next came cloth napkins, some forks, and out of the wine cellar, locked but I found the key on the frame above, a bottle of 1935 Pol Roger Champaign, with two fluted glasses. The bottle went into a bucket of ice.

The staff made noises like they were getting closer to the kitchen. My order almost complete, I searched for a pad of some kind and a pen in case I needed to have someone sign for this creation.

As the staff came in one door, I went out the other.

A short distance down the hallway brought me to the service elevator and I suddenly realized I didn't know what floor or what room she was in.

In addition, I couldn't very well go knocking on every door and also couldn't sashay out to the main desk in my present get up.

I rolled the cart into a closet, returned to the breakroom, changed back into my clothes, except for the shirt and the bow tie, and stashed the rest of the clothes and glasses in an empty locker.

Walking into the hallway I came face to face with one of the staff. A large fellow, who towered a head and a half taller than me, blocked my exit with a mop and a bucket of soapy water. He stood before me in a stained white gob shirt. His upper arm sported a big tattoo of an anchor with a sea serpent intertwined. Navy. I surmised he probably was keen at swabbing the deck.

"What are you doin' in here, yardbird?" His expression conveyed his displeasure of me being where I wasn't supposed to be.

"I'm looking for, Fred. He workin' tonight? Got a bet I need to collect and another one to place."

He crossed his arms and the anchor twitched. "Buddy, there's no Fred here."

"What?"

"I said —"

"I heard ya. Maybe you don't know him by Fred. Maybe he goes by another name here. Fred. Ya know? Little scrawny lad."

"We ain't got no Fred here."

I scratched the back of my head. "That little weasel. He said come to the kitchen at the Windsor and he'd settle out."

"This ain't the Windsor."

"It ain't?" I looked the hallway over. "These places all look the same to me. I heard they renovated—"

"I got work to do. I suggest you scram. Or do you want to get ugly about it?"

Looking one way and then the other, I lowered my voice and leaned in close. "Don't suppose you got a bookie here, do you? Save me from having to—"

He pointed at the door with the wet end of the mop. "Out!"

I gave him a sloppy salute, did as instructed, and made a beeline across the rug-covered floor for the front desk, centered in the opposite wall.

The skylighted atrium confirmed I was in fact traversing the impressive main lobby of the Brown Palace.

Behind the ornate front desk stood an ornate man. It was hard to tell if he indeed worked here or if a visiting dignitary from some foreign country had wandered back there looking for his key.

Since no one else needed his services at the moment, I took my chance and stepped up.

He stared at me blankly. "Yes?"

"Pencil and paper, please," I said through a smile.

He indicated with a nod a small desk and chair in a nook just beyond a potted plant, next to a shoe-shine stand.

With a nod of thanks, I walked over to said nook and inventoried the top of the desk. Hotel stationery, envelopes, and a pencil holder. Everything a man needed to send a nonsensical note. Pulling out the chair and glancing back at the potentate behind the front desk, who appeared to care less what I was up to, I sat.

With pencil in hand, I thought for a moment and peeled a sheet of stationery off the top of the stack. On it I scribbled:

> Dear lady,
> I don't know where you are.
> I hope this note finds you.

Period.

Pencil back in its place, I folded the stationery into three folds, slid it into an envelope, retrieved the pencil again, and wrote on the face of it:

Millicent Mundene

Pencil back in its place once more, I licked the glued flap and ran a knuckle over it to seal the deal.

Envelope in hand, I stood, then moseyed behind the potted plant to wait for the desk man to get busy.

A pimpled-faced bellhop walked briskly by, dressed in a uniform similar to the man at the desk, but with a drum-looking brimless cap. I decided this made him look like the potentate's junior general.

He glanced over at me, and I studied the leaves on the plant. Must have satisfied his curiosity because he didn't stop.

When the man behind the front desk looked sufficiently engaged, I crowded forward with, "Excuse me, excuse me," to the lady with her nose in the air and waved the envelope about. "Sir? Sir? Excuse me, ma'am. Sir?" To the potentate. "This is very important. Can you put it in her box?"

With a skillful balance of irritation toward me and not the family in front of him, he snatched it out of my hand and read the name.

Then he cocked his head in an odd way and looked at me with a condescending eye as if to say, 'what could possibly be so important from you to her?'

He turned and the envelope went into the box for room 517.

We had a winner!

Careful not to run into Navy with his mop and bucket, I made my way back to the breakroom, retrieved the rest of the waiter getup and glasses, then a minute later had my cart out of the closet.

A caged service elevator rattled my eye teeth all the way up to the fifth floor.

I opened the gate and set the cart in motion down the hall counting room numbers on the right-hand side along the way. To my left you could see down into the vast atrium.

At 517 my heart sank. A tray with the remains of her evening's meal mocked me from the floor.

But what was I thinking anyway? Obviously she hadn't ordered this wonderful snack I'd thrown together anyway. It was a bluff from the beginning.

What to do? What to do?

Years ago, I saw a guy hit in the head with a foul ball off the bat of the Kansas City Monarchs' 'Bullet' Rogan. Knocked him right outta his seat. That's about how I felt when the idea finally struck me.

Wrong floor. So obvious. I think the borrowed glasses had given me a headache.

I didn't really have to be there very long. Just needed enough time to see if she appeared in any way distressed. Like someone who might have a close relative missing. Nice and quick.

At least the tray on the floor let me know she was in. Then I wondered if a real kitchen staffer might wander up here to fetch said tray but dismissed the idea, figuring it would probably still be there in the morning.

Another wonder entered my head and my knuckles stopped about an inch from the door. Bellhops. How many did this hotel have? Did they appear on the floors every once in a while?

I had to get that thought out of my head. This was beginning to get more nerve racking, in the sense of being seen, than I had ever felt shadowing Sanderson.

Another thing gnawed at my gut. All the others had someone watching them. But I hadn't seen anyone in the lobby out of place and watching the elevators and stairs. Likewise, none on this landing. A good place to hide would be across the way, beyond the hotel's center chasm. No one peeking out of doors either. Then another thing. The tray had been set as a serving for two. Complications. Complications.

My knuckles finished their journey to the door of 517. Thought it best not to do shave and a haircut, two bits, and kept it simple. Three sharp raps.

While I waited, shave and a haircut, two bits, rattled through my brain and I tried to remember where I'd heard it first. In a song? A comedy skit? Perhaps....

"Yes? What do you want?"

Her voice brought me back to reality. It had the sound of a pretty teacher calling you out for falling asleep during a lecture. Nice and authoritarian at the same time. Her appearance did likewise. Very nice, but for some reason still dressed as if she might go to a nightclub at the drop of a hat. Auburn hair, form fitting red dress, stockings, and high heel shoes. Not my idea of relaxing in the room evening wear. Her nails were painted red and buffed to a shine. And makeup. A bit too much for my liking. Her perfume, a bit more tolerable. A sort of powdery mix of vanilla and orange.

I couldn't see past her but, because of the tray on the floor, I'd have bet a dollar to a donut she was not alone.

Which proved to be exactly the case as a man's voice came around her form from somewhere beyond my field of vision in the cavernous room.

She turned her head to look back and I noticed her hair was gathered in a low bun. The rest was waved on top. "You order more food? No?"

I held my head at a tilt. A, so she couldn't see my face very well. And B, so I didn't have to look through those nauseating spectacles.

Her attention returned to me, and I dropped my gaze to the floor and eyed the two champaign glasses. One with the mark of red lipstick and the other with some bubbly still in it, most likely flat and not bubbly.

"This is not ours." Her expression was an amalgamation of expressions in an amalgamated sort of way. Some folks seem to have a multitude of little muscles around their mouth and eyebrows to animate those expressions all the more. She was one of those.

Pulling a slip of paper from my inside jacket pocket, I consulted the blank form and read. "Say's here, 417."

She leaned out and tapped the door number with a painted nail. It went click, click, click. "517 here, you dolt."

Adjusting my glasses, I looked at the paper again. "No, 417. Oh!"

"You're obviously on the wrong floor."

Obviously. "Yes, ma'am, so I am." I stepped away until I felt the rail behind me before I turned the cart back toward the elevator. "Sorry to have disturbed you, ma'am. Chef has lousy handwriting." My chore complete, I pushed my way down the hall landing, but didn't hear the door close.

"Hey!"

One of her high heels sailed past my ear.

"Come back here a second!"

I thought the gig was up and held my breath.

"You got any crackers on there?"

I stopped in my tracks, released the cart, and turned.

She now stood in her stocking feet with the other shoe dangling by the strap from her index finger.

"Those Ritz ones. Not the soda crackers."

Feigning a survey of the cart, I shook my head. "Sorry, ma'am. No crackers. But I have olives and those little pickles."

She swiveled on her stocking feet and reentered the room. "I don't want little pickles, I want —"

The door slammed, cutting off her announcement of what she wanted. Then it opened again.

She stuck her head out and pointed past me.

I turned to look, then shrugged.

"My shoe, you dope. Bring me my shoe!"

# FIFTEEN

The funeral service for Norbert Olympus Bodie proved to be an interesting event. Held on the trading floor of the Mining Exchange, which at 15th and Arapahoe turned out to be in the same building where his offices resided on the sixth floor, the hoo-ha drew the Colorado bluebloods out of the woodwork. Anybody who was somebody made sure everybody knew they were there at N. O. Bodie's sendoff.

All, with the exception of the man of the hour N. O. Bodie who played hooky. No casket, no urn, and pardon the pun - no body.

The weather was uncooperative. Dark rain clouds had blown in an hour before and as everyone arrived the winds drove down the street faster than the Cadillacs. Thunder, lightning, and an airborne umbrella or two chased us all toward the main entrance, a massive stone arch which read 'EXCHANGE BUILDING', decorated with a life-sized bull's head on one side and a bear's head on the other.

High above, a twelve-foot-tall statue of a rugged, bearded prospector stood guard against the elements from its perch on the central tower of the Exchange. A sign of the times, the old sourdough held a large silver nugget which someone had plated gold in '35. His other hand leaned on the handle of a pickaxe.

The inclements however didn't stop every man who owned a tuxedo with a thousand dollars in his pocket from showing up and standing in front of the crowd to eulogize their old friend.

Said crowd sat under the thirty-foot ceiling in rows and rows of chairs in a sea of lady's hats. The men with fedoras, bowlers, and Stetsons had removed same out of respect.

On the front of these rows resided the tearful grandniece, Millicent Mundene. Dressed to the nines and sure to get her photo on the society page, she held dutifully to the arm of a much younger man.

I stood at the back of the room and always made sure to not wander into her line of sight. Even though I'd been dressed as help from the kitchen, she seemed a smart egg and I didn't want to take the chance.

Eventually one of the succession of orators clued us in on why N. O. Bodie had missed his own funeral. His last wishes were for his remains to be immediately loaded into a boxcar, on a train he had owned, and freighted not east to Bodie Island for his final resting place, but west to the old mining town of Bodie, California, in the Sierra Nevada Mountain range.

The history lesson of why this came to be sounded interesting in comparison to the several previous dull speeches. I leaned against the wall and lent an ear.

Our man of the hour had been born on Bodie Island in North Carolina. I remembered some of this from the obituary. It was originally known as Bodie's Island after his family emigrated from England on the HMS *Safety* in 1635. This heritage somewhat explained why Vyne and he were friends.

Bodie had arrived in Colorado in 1859, hot on the heels of gold seekers and fortune hunters. He not only staked a few claims, he also hired out other men to oversee a small manufacturing company. Bodie Iron Works became the first of many business ventures to follow, including foundries and mule trains.

The market for mining machinery was ripe for development and the company grew steadily. One of his innovations was to build the machinery in sections to ease the burden of transportation in the mountains.

The age of the automobile and electricity expanded his markets and branch offices to adjacent states. In 1909 he acquired his first truck, an '09 Randolph. In 1936 the Iron Works celebrated its 75th anniversary.

But Bodie's heart always returned to mining. From Colorado to California, he was more likely to be found underground than above.

A clap of thunder brought us all back to the trading floor as final words were said.

This had all been interesting, but not as interesting as what was to take place in the boardroom later in the evening.

# SIXTEEN

Her 'advisor' looked familiar. Either that or the fella she was hanging all over at the memorial earlier had a twin. Now he was pressed and polished, out of his tux and into a suit, briefcase in hand, smug look of 'I know more loopholes in the law than you have holes in your socks'. His trench coat and umbrella were tossed haphazardly at a clerk who'd been conscripted into active duty as a meeting helper of sorts.

Miss Mundene suddenly became Mrs. Mundene when she introduced him, the advisor - not the draftee, as her husband. No first name, just 'my husband'.

She had those high, high heels on again as she entered the sixth floor Mining Exchange board-room and made her way clickety-clack on the hard-wood floor all the way to the far end of the long table. The husband followed obediently a half step behind and, without offering to pull out her chair, promptly stepped to the adjacent one and sat.

She matched his move, sitting also, and folded her arms in front of her on the table. Her nails were a firetruck red and this matched both her lips and the red velvet suit she'd changed into. The accompanying flat crowned hat sported a brim which dwarfed the other ladies' hats in the room by a factor of three as did the white gardenias on the front.

From my vantage point, standing over by the rain-pelted windows, on the rounded corner end of the room, I now had a good view of all the participants who had trickled in earlier than the Fire Queen.

Arcadia Vyne, the current Chairman of the Board of the Mustang Gap Mining Company, major stockholder, and facilitator of the meeting, sat at the head of the table in a mahogany and brown leather chair, a long way opposite Millicent Mundene.

An inventory of the items in front of Vyne included a leather portfolio, a fountain pen, a drinking glass, carafe of water, a green glass banker's lamp, plus a small gavel. All the others at the conference table had the same, except for the gavel.

A wisp of a girl, smartly dressed, sat behind a small desk near the far corner where she could survey all the happenings. She held a stenographer's pad and pencil at the ready. A second pencil waited as backup behind her ear.

Under the three chandeliers, the room had the aroma of old cigars, old perfume, and old money. The obvious difference dependent on where you were in relation to who had what.

Working clockwise around the big, polished piece of mahogany office furniture, we had Gerald Myton in his white suit. At some point since the funeral, he'd changed from a black one. Elias Erdody sat next to Myton in a burgundy sport coat, then Holbrook Bahr, Mundene, the perfumiest of all the ladies, and hubby, the short Mr. and the tall Mrs. Cuthbert Preston III rounding on my side of the room, in mourning black, Bahr's elderly sister Thessaly Neufeld likewise, and back to Vyne.

Cuthbert Preston had entered with his hands in his pockets. Now he had them out under the table in his lap. Without putting one or the other on the edge, he awkwardly turned at the waist, adjusted his monocle, and stared at me.

I tipped my fedora.

This caused him to gulp and snap back to the forward position.

Introductions were made all around by Vyne 'for the record' and each nodded to indicate they matched the roll call. I was not introduced. For one - I was a nobody in this circle - and for two, we didn't want anyone to know I still breathed air on this side of the grave. The only person here who had seen me and knew me was Preston. I guess that's why he looked shocked.

We pretty much suspected Mundene to be the brains behind all this tomfoolery, but until she showed her hand, we had no proof.

I checked out the window and looked across through the wind-whipped rain to the top floor of the Belvedere Hotel. One building stood between us, its roof two floors below. It looked as though the roof had a drainage problem as a small pond was forming with bits of whatever you find on rooftops floating around like little boats in a hurricane.

If and when the hostages were found and freed, Rodrick was to hoof it to a room up in the Belvedere and give me the ol' window shade signal.

Nothing yet. The wind gusted rain and then let up just enough to see the hotel.

Vyne had told me he would try to draw this meeting out as long as possible, but since there were few items on the agenda, including the voting of the stockholders to approve dividends, he had a chore in front of him.

Problem was, no one was talking. No chit-chat, no murmuring, no idle gossip, no bringing up objections to the minutes from their last meeting. Nada.

I've been in meetings that seemed to go on for days because someone gets their motor running and can't seem to take their mouth out of gear. Usually begins with useless information and never gets to the point. Not this rich bunch. Even when Vyne tried to engage, they volleyed back shrugs.

Millicent Mundene and her one-man husband staff also sat silent as clams. But there was something about her face, in particular the right side of her lipsticked mouth. It twitched. She was itching to say something, but for some reason was holding back.

I decided right there and then she held all the cards. But what was her game? Arcadia Vyne loved to play games. Board games. Card games. Word games. This game – deadly. Lives depended on who came out winner.

It's hard to win a game when you don't know what the method of play is or what the tokens are capable of. We were like blind men in a maze waiting for someone to open a door.

The minutes continued to pass without comment.

I continued to check out the window without confirmation.

"Our next item, approval of the Company's shareholders of any and all dividends declared and paid or payable to any Company shareholder as of or prior to the Balance Sheet Date," stated Vyne.

Everyone eligible to vote nodded.

The right side of Millicent Mundene's mouth continued to twitch.

Visibly perturbed, Vyne huffed. "All in favor?"

All hands, except for the ineligible Mundene and Hubby's, rose.

"Opposed?"

None.

Vyne gaveled the table. "Approved."

He looked over at me and I shook my head. No signal yet.

"Is there any new business?"

"I," said Millicent Mundene coming alive with a

loud voice that echoed from one side of the room and back again, "have new business."

"Ah." Vyne drew out the sound. "As William Shakespeare penned in *King Henry IV*, 'The game is afoot.'"

I scratched the back of my head and whispered under my breath, "I thought I read that someplace else."

Mr. Mundene stood and cleared his throat. "As council for Mrs. Mundene I would like to present a proposition for all of you."

It was the voice from the Mundene hotel room.

Vyne pointed at him sternly with the gavel. "Mrs. Mundene will speak for herself. We do not recognize you. She is the heir of record to the holdings of N. O. Bodie. According to our bylaws, she is allowed to speak, but not you, sir." As his sentences grew longer, his voice grew louder, and he punctuated the end of his remarks with a tap of his bony index finger on the table. His voice echoed in the cavernous boardroom. I didn't know the skinny little man had it in him. In fact, since I'd known him, I'd never seen him this steamed.

The husband looked like he'd been slapped with a wet fish. He nervously opened his briefcase on the table in front of him and then with apparent second thoughts, clasped it back closed. "I beg the gentleman's pardon. Of course."

Millicent Mundene watched the exchange with a look of delight. Did she revel in seeing men put in their place? Time would tell.

She stood gracefully, managing to push her chair back with her thighs while moving upward. Slow. Methodical. A bit dramatic. "Ladies and gentlemen, I know I am here this evening as a simple observer. As the sole heir of my granduncle's estate there are many things I must attend to over a wide range of businesses and investments. Unfortunately, my granduncle, although a shrewd businessman over the years, left his legacy in near shambles due to hasty and poor decisions, made no doubt due to his declining health. He was a strong man. He was a stubborn man. He was used to getting his way. Well, it worked for a long, long time. But in the end it became a detriment."

I'll say one thing. She had the room.

After pausing a moment to make eye contact with each and every person at the big table, she took a step to the left and leaned forward, palms down. "I realize that we bid my granduncle farewell today and the soil hasn't begun to settle on his grave."

From where I stood window watch, I could see the side of her face and noticed a tear streaming down her cheek.

Holbrook Thompson Bahr gallantly stood and offered a handkerchief, which she promptly accepted.

"Thank you." Millicent Mundene held the white HTB monogramed cloth in both hands and dabbed the corner of her eye. "This is not a day for business." She tried to return it, but Bahr shook his jowls and held out a palm of refusal.

"Not a day for business. Not a day for business." She took a deep breath and smoothed herself down both sides, then patted her hair behind her ear and below the brim of her hat. "However, I've been shadowing Granduncle Bodie for the past few months, unable to convince him to refrain from disastrous decisions. Pleading with him to give me control and keep everything above water. His employees and you, the shareholders in this company, and perhaps others, didn't deserve what was happening."

Elias Erdody cleared his throat. "I had no idea!"

Gerald Myton nodded his agreement. 'We should have been told."

A look of confusion then crossed Erdody's face. "But our shares haven't lost value. The company appears sound."

"Sound on paper," Millicent Mundene said. "But not at its core. The Mustang Gap Mining Company has been on a land buying spree for the last nine or ten months. Depleting the coffers and gobbling up worthless claims all around the original mine. A multitude of mines played out a decade ago. My granduncle managed to do so with the help of his company manager. Discreetly." She paused. "If this information becomes public knowledge the share prices will plumet. Pennies on the dollar."

A peal of thunder, as if timed, rattled the chandeliers.

"But this...this is ridiculous." Thessaly Neufeld looked at the silent Vyne. "Arcadia, is this possible?"

He contemplated for a moment. "I'm not sure. This is all sudden and unexpected information."

I knew better. If Vyne didn't know about it, it didn't happen. No, he was trying to figure out why she was spinning this yarn. The reason I knew better was because while watching the lady Mundene out of one eye, I was watching him out of the other and had picked up on him subtly shaking his head from side to side.

Something stunk, but I'd have to leave it to him to take action as my job was to watch the window across the way, which I did every so often. No flapping. More rain. More lightning. I returned a slight head shaking back to him.

He pursed his lips. He's not a happy man when he does that.

I surveyed the expression of everyone who faced me, and they were all the same. Blank with eyes looking this way and that. It was as if suddenly no one in the room trusted anybody else. They all had one thing in common, with the exceptions of Vyne and Millicent Mundene, they all had a loved one or at least someone close to them missing and in danger.

❦

To backtrack a bit, this is why I was peering out the parted curtain so often to try and spy the flapping window shade.

Earlier in the day, before the rain set in, but after we had determined that Millicent Mundene had no skin in the game as far as a missing person, Vyne decided to revisit all the other shareholders' neighborhoods for us to get a better look at who was watching who.

At our second stop, Myton's. We spotted him.

Sanderson.

Our next step was to trick Mr. Loud Tie into thinking Myton's son Arthur had somehow escaped from wherever he needed to escape from.

The theory being that Sanderson would hotfoot it to said escaped location to see how it happened, and thus lead us to all the hostages.

Sanderson wasn't born yesterday. He was born the day after that. He fell and he fell hard.

Once again Baylee played his part as a cab flew up to the curb in front of the Myton mansion and he jumped out, ran to the door, on which he banged his fist while yelling, "Dad, it's me. It's me, Arthur. I've escaped!"

When Gerald Myton opened the door, of course he knew it wasn't his son, but Baylee quickly conveyed to him to get in on the act. Myton in turn started patting him on the back and hugging him so as to keep Baylee's face hidden. After much slapping and hugging they went inside and closed the door.

Seconds later, Sanderson sped by like a roadrunner chasing his next meal. We followed and with Rick now behind the wheel almost didn't keep up. Miles added to miles as we left the city toward the mountains. Eventually we arrived right behind him at the most obvious of places - the Mustang Gap Mining Company's Mine #1.

Sanderson nearly came out of his Dodge before it stopped rolling. He ran into the mine and a few minutes later came out with a face I recognized. Gus, the goon from the printing room in Laramie.

With a lot of hand flailing, apparently he convinced Sanderson that Arthur Myton remained inside and had never left the premises.

Sanderson removed his hat and scratched his head. He didn't have enough brain cells to figure this one out. However, by the way he ran back to his car and spun it around in the dirt, I figured he knew someone who did.

Rick managed to back us up a side road just in time to watch the coupe go by.

"What now?" I asked Vyne.

"This is a matter for the police. Time to bring Detective Raft up to speed."

❦

The speed at which Detective Raft did come up to said speed surprised us all. Without hesitation he called out Seargent Griz Asher and a bunch of his men, instructing them to weaponize themselves. The location of the Mustang Gap Mine #1 was outside Raft's jurisdiction, so he made a call to the state police, cautioning them it was to unofficially be his collar. We sent Mr. Rick with them with instructions to return to the Belvedere Hotel, go up to the top floor of rooms, find one facing the Mining Exchange and break the door down if necessary to go in and flap the shade. A sign all the hostages were free, and we could play our hand.

✺❊✿❧

Of course, Millicent Mundene knew of none of this. She had no idea her man Sanderson was about to earn a set of police bracelets. She had no idea her leverage was in the process of being unleveraged. And without all that important knowledge, knowledge which would have been so helpful in her negotiations, she proceeded with the plan she came into the room with.

But without the flapping shade, we had to let her go on with her show.

Plus, we really wanted to know what she was going to do with all those phony stock certificates.

# SEVENTEEN

I thought I knew where this was heading but thinking and knowing can be two different things. And thinking and knowing were certainly two different things on this evening in the boardroom atop the Mining Exchange Building.

All that needed to happen was for that shade to flap and the gig would be up on Millicent Mundene. As soon as I got my signal, I'd give the high sign to Vyne, and he'd bring her down like a house of cards.

Cuthbert Preston had finally brought his right hand out from under the table, and I could see it still sported the thin leather glove. He appeared to fish for something in his jacket pocket, hard to tell looking at his back, but my suspicion proved valid as he turned away from his wife and scribbled something on a piece of paper with a pen.

Millicent Mundene rapped on the long table and brought everyone's attention back to her. "However, I have some information that is going to turn the Mustang Gap Mining Company around tomorrow."

"What!" Thessaly Neufeld gasped and leaned back in her chair.

As you all know, Gerald Myton's son is the Chief Geologist for Mustang Gap Mining. He's been down in Mine #1 doing some testing in a new sublevel shaft."

"Arthur hasn't said anything to me about this." Gerald Myton looked like someone who'd just been told his mother wasn't his real mother.

She glanced at her husband. "Let's just say, Arthur and I have become close friends." Her husband lowered his head.

"And what then, is this new information? Has my son found something?"

"He's calling it the 'Mother Lode'."

Myton slapped the table with the palm of his

hand so hard that Evangeline Preston jumped in her seat. "Why, that's fantastic!"

I looked at Vyne. He didn't appear to think it fantastic.

The Professor slowly raised his hand. "Excuse me, Mrs. Mundene. This is not official information. We haven't been told anything. I'm not aware that management has been told anything. We're going to need some verification —"

She tilted her head back and laughed a big laugh. When she'd composed herself she walked around to Vyne and stood behind him so that he had to look over his shoulder.

"No one has this information, except me. I've told Arthur to keep it under his hat." She moved around behind Cuthbert Preston, and he tapped the table with his gloved hand.

She glanced down and he pushed the piece of paper a bit with his finger.

Vyne saw it too and coughed a loud cough. "Mrs. Mundene, this is most irregular."

This managed to draw her attention away from the little paper and back to the group.

"I don't agree," she said after a long pause.

Now I was getting confused. She'd been getting the inside pitch from Arthur, and then she had him kidnapped. This didn't make sense. Unless.... Unless he let himself be kidnapped.

She moved on from Preston and continued her circumnavigation of the room. "I want this to all be official. So, you are all going to vote this evening to release this information to the public tomorrow at noon."

"Nonsense." This from Erdody.

"I think your little sister, Ava is her name, no? I think little Ava might like you to reconsider."

The cat was out of the proverbial bag now.

"And if we don't?"

"Oh, I'll just leak it anyway. Tomorrow at noon the world will know that the Mustang Gap Mining Company has found the biggest vein of gold in the Rockies since 1889. But none of those precious loved ones of yours will be around to read the headlines."

Erdody stood. Young in relation to most of the Denver business establishment, he threw back his chair into the wall and charged around to her.

Hubby Mundene didn't appear in any way chivalrous as he never looked up.

As Erdody came nose to nose with her, she let out that awful laugh again. Sounded like a couple of hyenas with their tails tied together.

Erdody stamped his foot.

She raised a hand and pointed a painted finger-nail at his nose. "Go sit down. I want this all legal." She looked over at the secretary, "You getting this all down, sweetie?"

I checked the window again.

No flapping shade. What if Arthur Myton had fouled the works?

Erdody stood firm. "I don't see what difference it makes."

She pointed at Hubby. "We have papers drawn up attesting to the fact that you are all in agreement to release this information at noon tomorrow. You will vote and you will sign."

Erdody continued to stand his ground. "What have you to gain? If this is announced tomorrow or next week? Whenever it is, the news will certainly drive up the price of the company stock. You will profit." He waved an arm to include everyone at the table, "We all will profit."

"Oh, but you won't."

"You're not making any sense."

"Go back and sit, airplane man."

This brought utter silence to the room.

A glance at the secretary confirmed her pencil had stopped and her head had tilted an ear.

All the while the two stood their ground with each other.

I could tell Vyne was working on the problem.

When he raised his head and smiled at me, I knew he had it.

Wish I had it.

She took a step toward Elias Erdody, and he flinched and gave ground. He'd metaphorically crashed and burned. His whole body took on a look of defeat as he retreated to his seat.

Millicent Mundene followed him as far as Vyne. She reached around him and took the gavel. "Call for the vote."

He surveyed each of the occupants of the table with his eyes.

I'll note that, except for Hubby, slash councilor, Mundene, each expression I could see relayed surrender.

All but Arcadia Vyne.

"Mr. Bodie held the vote for his shares. As all legalities are yet to be resolved, you have no vote on this matter and it will be recorded as an abstain from Norbert's estate. Do you understand?"

Hubby Mundene fielded the question. "Yes, she understands."

"Very well." The Professor stood and looked

over at the secretary in the corner. "Of course, we are doing this under duress, and it will all be recorded in the minutes."

Neither Mundene nor husband batted an eyelash.

That's when I figured out what Vyne was on to. She didn't care. This was all a ruse to cover up something more sinister. If not, she'd have made sure the secretary didn't record anything. Or…maybe the secretary was in on it. Or…maybe they planned to ambush her and substitute their own notes. Come to think of it, I didn't have it yet. Was Mundene so audacious to think this would work?

Then it came to me.

If there were no big strike then it stood to reason that in a day or two, after the announcement, all this would come crashing down and the stock rendered worthless.

The Professor stood straight, disdain on his face, and said, "As per our by-laws, but with duly recorded reservations, I call for a vote to release the news of a major strike in Mine #1 —"

"To be worded by me," Millicent Mundene said loudly from her seat, to which she had just returned.

Vyne sighed. "To be worded by Mrs. Mundene. Also, per our by-laws, the vote will be called by order of the largest shareholder to the least."

They locked glares.

I took the opportunity to step a few steps toward the table, lean on Cuthbert Preston's shoulder, and say, "Excuse me." I reached for a glass and a pitcher of water, and snagged his note which went directly into my pocket. "I'm parched."

Millicent Mundene didn't give me as much as a glance.

"Get on with it!" Since she had, for all intents and purposes, taken control, she had lost all civility and good manners, not that she had a lot to begin with. "You're the biggest shareholder. Cast your vote."

He smiled. "You are mistaken, Mrs. Mundene. I am no longer the largest shareholder. This afternoon, I sold all my shares to Mr. Cooper, the man by the window, for the sum of one dollar. Now, having done so and owning no interest in the Mustang Gap Mining Company, I resign as Chairman of the Board."

She turned her head to me, and I knew as she did so, my name was coming to the forefront of her mind. To this point in the evening, I'd just been the man by the window. Now, I had become the man who shouldn't be here. The man who should still be locked up in the not very deep and not very wide cell in the former Wyoming Territorial Prison.

I smiled and waved at her. "How do you do?"

If steam could ever come out of a woman's ears, this would have been a great time to bring out the circus calliope. We would have had music for days.

She took a deep breath and regained her composure. "Very well, then Cooper can cast the first vote."

Hubby Mundene had taken a document out of his briefcase and with a pen it looked like he crossed something off, probably Vyne's name, and written something in its place. Probably mine.

"Can't," I said from the window. "Those by-laws. Have you read them? I brushed up after lunch. Even though I am now the largest stockholder, I am not Chairman of the Board. Mr. Vyne has resigned from that position. It now falls, according to the by-laws, to the next person who has been on the board the longest, as an interim, until a special vote can be called to elect a new Chairman. All of the major stockholders are in the room, and I am low man on the totem pole. Only the Interim Chairman can call for a vote."

The secretary in the corner looked up and her expression seemed to say, 'That's a new one on me.'

Mundene seethed and looked around the table. "And who might that be? Speak up!"

"I believe, it falls to Mr. Myton," I said.

Gerald Myton stood and nervously cleared his throat. "Mr. Cooper, as Interim Chairman of the Board, may I ask you —"

"For his vote, you idiot! For his vote." Millicent Mundene was coming unglued. "Largest shareholder votes, etc. etc. Get on with it."

Myton moved away from his chair and approached me slowly. "Mr. Cooper may I ask if you have a dollar?"

I pulled my wallet from my jacket. Sure enough I had several. "Why yes, Mr. Myton, I do."

"Would you by chance, by a gentlemen's handshake agreement, like to purchase all of my shares in the Mustang Gap Mining Company?"

I handed him the dollar. "Why, yes I would like that very much." We shook the deal done.

He turned on his heels to face Millicent Mundene. "I resign my position of Interim Chairman of the Board."

For a woman with so much steam ready to come out of her ears, she composed herself again and eyed the remainder of the shareholders. "Who's next in line?"

Erdody stood. "I believe I am."

He walked around the table to me. I handed him a dollar out of my wallet. We shook on it, and he said, "I resign."

Next came Holbrook Bahr. Dollar exchanged. Hand shook. Resignation.

Then his sister.

When Evangeline Preston stood, she did so with class. Any young girl, perhaps even the secretary in the corner who now took business notes, might take personal etiquette notes as well. If, that is, she wanted to study the art of standing with grace and composure. Evangeline Preston held her head high, raised her hand, and crooked her index finger in my direction with an unspoken, 'come hither young man.' Textbooks would be written about this moment.

I hithered around the table and handed her my last George Washington.

"I resign," she said. "As I believe there are no more board members, the Board is dissolved." With a broad smile, she dropped to her seat. Textbooks would not record that.

Suddenly Cuthbert Preston stood on his chair,

apparently to get a head taller than she, and yelled, "I object!" As he did so, his monocle popped loose and landed on the table. He pointed the gloved hand at the ceiling. "I object!"

Of course!

I pulled the note from my pocket.

Scrawled by the man who'd cut his hand in Laramie:

Millicent, the man by the window is Cooper. Vyne's Man. He's escaped! What do we do?

# EIGHTEEN

The man who'd tripped near the old prison cells and fell on the tin. The voice I couldn't place at the time.

Cuthbert Preston III?

That mouse of a man?

Mrs. Preston immediately put her hand to her forehead and swooned. This confirmed I wasn't the only one surprised.

The big boardroom atop the Mining Exchange erupted into chaos.

I moved to try and catch the falling woman and managed to slide on the floor in time to cradle her head above the hardwood. In the process her legs swung about and kicked the chair out from under her husband, still standing on it with his hand in the air. He promptly toppled off and landed on me.

The Professor, in the meantime, had taken my place at the window and he must have seen a flapping shade, because he shouted out, "They've got them. They're free!"

At the far end of the room, a boot kicked the double doors open and Griz Asher, occupant of said boot, barreled in with Sanderson cuffed to his arm.

The secretary in the corner screamed and her steno pad flew into the air.

Detective Raft entered behind his sergeant and made a beeline for the Mundenes. Hubby Mundene grabbed his wife by the arm and attempted to make a run for it but was slowed as she tried to kick off her high heels. Eventually they gathered some steam and were able to sidestep Griz Asher due to the thug anchored to his wrist.

Raft, about as athletic as a rhino, made a grab at the fleeing duo and missed.

I passed off Mrs. Preston's head to the cradling hands of Holbrook Bahr and set after them. Out of the corner of my eye I saw Asher transfer his half of the cuffs to the knob of one of the big doors.

In front of me, the Mundenes were heading for the descending stairs, but at the last possible moment, Mrs. Mundene put a hand in the back of Mr. Mundene and sent him headfirst down the flight to the left. In turn she altered her trajectory and ascended to the right.

I didn't wait for the scream to end from below but followed her up.

Griz Asher's big boots sounded behind me.

The marble steps met a landing and a door rattled to my right. Though it more stairs, these wooden, led to another door, which in turn dumped me out onto the roof of the Mining Exchange into the thunderstorm. Just above I spotted the statue of the prospector and his gold-plated silver nugget.

The wind nearly took me off my feet. Across the rooftop, in the direction of the Belvedere Hotel, Millicent Mundene peered over the edge. She held a hand on the top of her big hat for a moment, then a gust in her face pulled it free and it sailed past me and adhered itself on Griz Asher's chest.

He was not amused.

With nowhere to go but over, she pulled herself up onto the building's top ledge. Her auburn hair whipped about and plastered in wet strands to her face.

"Stop!" I yelled into the wind. "Don't do something crazy!"

She crooked her knees, desperately trying to balance against the gusts of wind.

Lightning flashed.

She kept looking over her shoulder and then back at us.

The sergeant and I crept forward until we were about two steps away from her.

"I'll get all of you for this!" The wind carried her threat through the rain to us. "Vyne..., you...," she pointed and snarled, "the whole lot. I'll make all of you regret—"

Lightning flashed down from the heavens and struck the statue on the brim of its hat and for a moment its whole body seemed to glow a greenish hue.

Startled by the strike, Mundene stood on the ledge, mouth agape. The wind ceased for a fraction of a moment and the weight she'd been using to resist it countered her balance and she disappeared over the side just as the clap of thunder from the lightning strike to the old prospector's hat slapped us back.

# Nineteen

**Griz** Asher and I looked at each other. Rain drenched, we covered the two steps to where Millicent Mundine had disappeared over the edge and the wind smacked us in the face.

Out of reach, within what seemed to be about ten feet, the wind caught her back and just sort of held her there. For a moment I thought she might blow up and into our arms.

The wind had other ideas and cartwheeled her about for a second or two, then dropped her into the shallow pond of water on the rooftop below.

Splash!

Through the rain, all I saw were red ripples in the roof pond and it took a moment for my brain to realize it wasn't blood, but her clothes.

Griz Asher let out a whistle. "Did you get a load of that twisting backward swan dive? Is she dead?"

"I can't tell from here. We better get down there—"

"Hey, I think she's movin'!"

Asher was right.

Millicent Mundene had survived the fall. She rolled over on her hands and knees, stood, then wobbled over to a vent pipe to steady herself. Pushing wet hair off her face, she made for the roof access door.

"I don't believe it. The circus must be in town. Did you see what that dame just did?" Ever the cop, Asher turned from the ledge and headed back the way we came. "Maybe we can get to the street before her."

As Griz Asher and I raced back down the stairs we were blocked by the group of folks tending to Hubby Mundene. He stood on unsteady legs on the landing. Holbrook Bahr and his sister, Thessaly Neufeld, were trying to calm him while the secretary from the corner attempted to put what appeared to be his broken arm into a makeshift sling.

We yelled a, "Clear a path!" and parted the throng enough to get through and eventually made our way to the ground floor and out onto the street. The rain still poured, and the wind still blew, as we swam more than ran to the entrance of the Belvedere.

Asher grabbed the doorman by the sleeve of his jacket. "Hey. You see. A. Dame?" He fought to catch his breath. "A dame come out. Of that door? Down there?" He pointed toward the entrance of the building between the Belvedere and the Mining Exchange. "Red. Dress?"

"As a matter of fact. She did."

I also was gulping air and rain, even though we were up under the awning. "Where'd? She go?"

The doorman stood mum - hand out, palm up.

"For, Pete's sake." I dug into my front pants pocket and found lint. "Asher. You got any dough?"

He looked at me with incredulity. "On my pay?"

"This guy's deaf and dumb." I felt around in my jacket pockets.

"I got a cure for that!" The big sergeant grabbed the doorman by the back of his collar and lifted him off the ground. "Spill!"

The doorman spilled. Millicent Mundene had stumbled out the door and turned in his direction.

Then, he said, she'd trudged down the sidewalk past him until she was out of sight in the rain.

Gone.

❦

At the police station the big sergeant and I pushed our way into the crowded main lobby. Glad to be out of the rain, we searched for a cup of hot coffee each and surveyed the happenings.

Holbrook Bahr and his sister sat over by the far wall with Hubby Mundene between them. He cradled his arm and winced from time to time.

Detective Raft had Arthur Myton handcuffed and held on to him by his elbow. Gerald Myton stood at a nearby desk on a phone, tapping his foot and trying to wake his lawyer.

Another officer babysat the also handcuffed Cuthbert Preston.

The rest were assorted wet kidnap victims reuniting with wet family.

Rowena Preston, a good head taller than her mother, Evangelina, cried a waterfall of tears which dripped down to mix with the puddles of rainwater tracked in by everyone.

Arcadia Vyne stood at the counter and was giving a statement to the desk sergeant.

Raft passed off Arthur to yet another policeman and moved in beside Vyne to offer details and fill in the gaps from his perspective of the evening.

The only party guest I didn't see was Sanderson. His loud tie was more than enough to get an invite to model a shiny set of silver bracelets. But alas, absent. Disappointing to say the least.

Baylee, Rick, and Stewart came in through the main doors accompanied by a roll of thunder, circled me, and erased my thoughts of the guy with the ugly neckwear as they asked me to bring them up to speed.

"Man, oh man," said Baylee. "They've got half of Denver in here. Who they arrestin'?"

Stewart whistled. "We hear you own all the stock in the Mustang Gap Mining Company now."

"Well, not all of it. But the most for sure."

"How's it feel to be a wealthy man?" Baylee tipped his chauffeur's cap at me and water dripped in my shoe.

"First thing I'm gonna do," I said as I put my thumbs under my armpits and puffed out my chest, "is buy some dry socks. Then I'll wait for Mary to get out of the hospital and take her to the Cosmopolitan for that Waldorf salad. Not Dutch this time. My treat all the way."

Someone gruffly cleared their throat behind me. With a tug on the sleeve of my wet jacket, Griz Asher pulled me backward and leaned to whisper in my ear. "We need you down in the lineup room."

"That cave? Who's we?"

"Don't ask. Got somebody we need you to pick out of a lineup."

Curiosity sometimes gets me in trouble.

He crooked an index finger and headed for the door. "This way."

I shrugged and said to the boys, "Be back soon." Parking my empty coffee cup on a table, I followed Asher.

The lineup room seemed even damper after the storm.

I heard spurs jingle.

Deputy Beuford Warner in a big white hat stood next to the door.

"Evening. What are you doing here?"

He raised a knee and put a boot back on the wall. "Came to make sure I get to take that so-and-so back to Laramie once this lot's done with him."

My eyes adjusted to the brightly lit wall at the end of the room where I expected to see eight or eleven mugs of similar looks. To my surprise, just one man stood solo.

"What gives?"

Griz Asher pointed at Sanderson. "Need you to pick him out of that conga line."

Wondering if it might be a trick question, I covered the steps over to the ugly mug and stood toe-to-toe with him.

Asher stayed back in the shadows. "You can verify that as the man who put Mary Smith in the hospital." Statement, not question.

"I can."

Sanderson smirked.

I still had the urge to educate him as to how he shouldn't have done it. "Why'd you have to put a fist in the middle of Mary's face?"

He spit on my lapel. "No dame ain't ever gonna' kick my ankle like she did and call me a 'miscreant'.

"Do you even know what that means?"

"Go fry an egg."

"Now, I'm going to tell you this in a friendly way...."

At that point the lights went out, putting us all in the dark. When they came back on, I caught a glimpse of the big sergeant's hand coming away from the switch.

"How'd that happen, you suppose?" he asked the deputy.

I looked down and found the bulk of Sanderson's tie gathered in my grip with his body on the floor and his head just inches above due to my holding it up by the ugly material.

Believe it or not, Griz Asher smiled. "What's that lowlife's beef with the librarian calling him a 'miscreant'?"

"I can't imagine," offered Deputy Warner.

A throat cleared and it belonged to Detective Raft. "What's going on here, Cooper?" He pointed what looked to be a new pipe at Sanderson's limp form.

"Well, it seems the lights went out," I replied. "This joker here tripped. Loose shoelaces. On the way to the floor the misfortunate mug appears to have blackened his eye, spit out a tooth, cracked a rib, and bruised a rib. Fortunately, I was able to keep him from hitting his head." I released the tie. "For a moment, anyway."

The detective turned his attention to the sergeant. "Storms always have done funny things to the lights down here. Be glad when we get to move to the new jail."

"Yes, sir."

"Cooper, I'd get those knuckles bandaged if I were you. Sanderson's face did a real job on 'em."

A puff of smoke exited the bowl of the pipe. "Very well." He pointed to the villainous lump on the floor and nodded toward Asher and Warner. "You two good with this?"

The Colorado lawman and the Wyoming lawman nodded their agreement.

"Looks like things are under control. Get somebody down here to take out the trash." With that he turned and left.

# TWENTY

Millicent Mundene had disappeared.

Inspector Raft surmised she'd left town.

Arcadia Vyne agreed, and his face never revealed what he thought about her stormy rooftop threat when I told him.

He did, however, express his displeasure at my last encounter with Sanderson. "You can't be judge and jury, Jonas," he said.

After a bit of soul searching, I knew he was spot on and agreed to go forward after the next Sunday sermon to get things right. I'd let my anger get the best of me. Lesson learned.

Another player in this game did a bit of confessing too as it didn't take long for Cuthbert Preston to spill what he knew, and we were all amazed to find out he was the brain behind the operation. Well mostly, until Millicent Mundene came on board.

❦

A day later, Baylee, Stewart, Rodrick, and I were practicing our chess moves in Arcadia Vyne's game room. We had to keep our skills up as at any given time Vyne, currently down in his laboratory working on his latest tea blend, might appear and challenge us to a game.

We were surrounded by paintings of cats. Carvings of cats. Cat figurines. Cat frescos and tapestries of Egyptian hairless cats. Above the fireplace an oil portrait of Vyne's late wife, cat on lap.

Baylee and I sat opposite one chess board, while the other two men occupied another of the twenty-one tables in the semicircular room. Not all contained chessboards, but an interesting mix of other games from *Mahjong* to checkers.

Caffeine, the feline in charge of this part of the mansion, slept in her overstuffed wingback chair. Light from one of the floor to ceiling windows streamed onto her and she purred in the warmth.

"I don't get what the scam was," said Baylee as he contemplated his next move.

"The press operation at the big house in Laramie was the center of the whole ordeal." I winced as he slid his bishop into a bad spot. "Preston the idea man, Mundene the organizer, and Sanderson and his crew the counterfeiters and kidnappers."

"What was Mr. Preston thinking?" asked Rodrick from nearby. "Surely he didn't need the money."

"A little background might help," I said. "Seems Preston had found a man who could make a reasonable looking copy of a share of the Mustang Gap Mining Company stock certificate. It didn't have to be perfect because the plan was to send the bogus money diplomas to different cities around the country and revive the old bucket shops."

"Bucket shops?" asked Stewart.

"Yeah, those shops had mostly disappeared in the '20s, but they seem to be making a comeback. The setup is that the bucketeers concentrate on pigeons who want to wager on the price of stocks. The kicker this round being the plan to cause a premature leak and release of the news that the Mustang Gap Mine had struck the mother lode. Greed assured there would be gamblers ripe for the picking and an easy mark to unload the worthless paper."

"The certificates printed in Wyoming." Baylee slowly took his hand from the bishop.

"Exactly." I moved a pawn with my bandaged hand. "Said release hinging on Millicent Mundene's manipulation of the board meeting by having Sanderson and his goons kidnap the loved ones of all the key stockholders."

"Then why did they grab you?"

"While I didn't qualify as a loved one of Arcadia Vyne, the fact I was associated with him had to do. You all know his sister in the Sanatorium is in no shape to be moved."

"This Mundene lady," said Rodrick. "Wasn't she in line to inherit?"

"Yeah, but she couldn't take a chance that she might not be in ol' N. O. Bodie's last will and testament. Even if she were, she stood to make more money in a week by selling the fake stock as she would in the dividends from an inheritance. The anticipated headlines in all the big city papers practically guaranteed it. I think she tried to create a modern-day gold rush of a different kind. Also, the phony stock announcement all but guaranteed the stock to tank in a few days."

"Crafty bird."

"You said it, Rick. By the time everyone with a supposed claim got sorted like chaff from the legitimate owners, she planned to be long gone leaving a mess to tie up the courts for years."

"So back to my original question," said Rodrick. "What was Mr. Preston thinking? Why the scheme?"

"The little guy really wanted it all to get into a pile. We found out he held a grudge against some of the other major stockholders and he saw it as a way to foul up their life while at the same time getting out from under the thumb of that overbearing wife and daughter of his."

Silent Stewart, who'd been quietly moving his chess pieces grinned. "He and his partners in crime almost pulled it off. Check!"

"What?" Rodrick scratched his noggin and eyed the board. "How did...."

"They almost did," I agreed. "Almost."

Rodrick stood and walked around his table and stood to look over Stewart's shoulder at the board.

"As it stands," I continued, "the phony certificates should have been intercepted by now and they'll all be destroyed. The strike, which in fact does exist, will be announced in due course, and everyone can get back to life as usual. That is, except the crooks, and of course Millicent Mundene."

"They still haven't found her?" asked Baylee as he also stood and walked over to study the other chessboard.

"Nope. She literally disappeared in the wind."

"About the strike. How do you know it's real?"

"Arthur Myton," I said. "He's a geologist. He had originally confirmed it and instead of telling his dad, who he doesn't get along with, he took the news to Preston. Playing both ends against the middle. Preston told Millicent Mundene no strike existed."

"Boy, talk about a double cross!"

Arthur was the inside man as far as the kidnap victims went. His job was to keep an eye on them and sabotage any escape attempts."

"What about Mrs. Preston?" Rodrick appeared to have conceded eventual defeat in his match. "And Rowena?"

"I figure Mrs. Preston and daughter will probably decide not to weather the scandal and will eventually put their house up for sale. Most likely, they'll leave the state. Her bank account held all the cash. Preston wanted it all to himself."

Rodrick watched as Stewart set up the board

again. "For a moment, there in the boardroom," he said, "you were the major stockholder of the Mustang Gap Mining Company and a very wealthy man."

"At least on paper," I agreed. "With my new-found fortune, I had dreams of buying the Preston's mansion and becoming Arcadia Vyne's neighbor instead of living over the carriage house."

"Oh, no you didn't!" Baylee laughed and moved a knight, but I stared it back.

"Oh, yes I did. My early mornings to be spent drinking coffee, no tea allowed, in my spacious backyard and yelling, 'Toodle-oo and nonesuch' over the hedge at the lot of you. But being the good Joe I am, I traded it all back to the original owners for the original dollar bills I'd paid. And all those grateful millionaires to a T left me with a couple of shares to call my own. At least I'll be able to take Mary Smith out in style when she's released from the hospital."

"How many, may I ask, are a few shares?" This from Rodrick.

"I assume the same amount they gave all of you."

He didn't seem surprised. "Enough that I don't have to work if I choose, but I choose to work anyway. You?"

"Yes."

"Stewart?"

He nodded the affirmative.

"Baylee?"

The young chauffeur drew a breath and moved the knight back to his first choice. "Checkmate!"

Arcadia Vyne
will Return
in

# The Case
of
the
Baffling Case

by

Ira Amos

# James Kay Publishing
## PO Box 470733
## Tulsa, Oklahoma 74147

This Arcadia Vyne Mystery

# Bad News

## on

## the

# Doorstep

is also available at

**www.jameskaypublishing.com**

Made in the USA
Coppell, TX
07 December 2024